AF140884

ALEX TROY

NEAR EAST THE STARS BEGIN

as Does Betrayal

novum ⬛ pro

This book is also available as e-book.

© 2024 novum publishing

ISBN 978-3-7116-0095-0
Editing: Philip Kelly
Cover photos: Houchi,
Ig0rzh I Dreamstime.com
Cover design, layout & typesetting:
novum publishing
Author's illustration: Alex Troy

www.novum-publishing.co.uk

Print product with financial
climate contribution
ClimatePartner.com/16547-2311-1001

AMERICA THROUGH THE LOOKING GLASS
A SPY THROUGH A PEEPHOLE
SEES TRICKS PLAYED ON PEOPLE

So he double crosses
his girl and his bosses,
and tries to disarm
hegemons that cause harm
His girl has the brains
to keep him in chains.

By uniting the earth
he plans Nature's rebirth.
but gets a bang on the head
in Iran; and well nigh dead
finds truth is revealed
and the world can be healed.

CHAPTER ONE

Every morning is the same. The moon gracefully retires. Dawn waits in silence until muezzin then flings open her windows and gazes out upon a spotless sky and the world of men below. Serene and bright, the day glazes the lands with a sheen that makes them irresistible.

Yet sometimes I long for the sounds of Wenlock, the susurration of the grass; the rustling hedges the lamentation of the wind in those majestic trees, which sway and dance, in time with one another. And above them a glorious ever changing English heaven, where clouds of alabaster walk the skies, like ladies decked in grey and white, and I, hardly breathing for joy, re-enter Paradise.

Yet here every dawn delights me. God, in Islam, is the Lord of Dawn.

My first job was in PR. I didn't like it. Confused and frustrated, I ran away to India. We pretend humanity is one. But India is a myriad in which extraordinary differences are revealed. It has a precious integrity more than the sum of its parts. This integrity prevents disintegration.

In those early days we stole into Shamalaji and saw a thousand tribes gather and were honoured to learn of Bhrahma who created the world, after he was brought into being by the one who, every moment, creates thousands of universes, and destroys thousands. I mean of course Lord Vishnu. In the last days holy Narsimh Mehta wrote prayers in honour of Shri Krishna, and from them came Mahatma's prayer.

So, I discovered Gandhi, a lawyer who freed India without shooting my dad in the back. He gave birth to a new humanity. He inspired me. India is the home of spiritualism. Spirits reside there. They survive invasions, tyrannies, famines.

Mother Nature, neglected across the world, is failed by religion, which serves men at her expense, save for Ambaji who serves her.

In India those who work the earth know the story of Ambaji. Her body dismembered, her heart fell like a meteor to the ground. In Bhadra Purnima they come to her shrine under a full moon. They hear readings of her verses, and worship her, and learn how her hand in marriage was accepted by Lord Shiva.

A great fair is organised in her honour.

Her heart, the meteor, fell to earth. A triangular Vishwa Yantra, inscribed with figures and the syllable 'Shree' in the centre, represent her deity. There is no idol, which testifies antiquity. The full moon of Bhadrapad is one of the most holy days. Farmers come to a place that takes its name from the Goddess. The fair, held on full moon days, holds drama in the evenings. Bhavai, and Garba are organised. The devout attend readings of the Saptashati, the seven hundred verses in praise of the goddess, and worship her temple. Her hand is accepted in holy marriage by Lord Shiva and celebrated by all who flock there. Men once danced the Garbi after victory. They danced to couplets and amorous songs sung by the Charanswar, and through worship they dance for those who work the land and who swear by love and family.

They honour Saptapadi, the seven steps brides and grooms take round the fire. The groom sings, "With God as our guide, let us nourish each other grow together; preserve wealth; share joys and sorrows, have and care for children, be together forever remain lifelong friends and as two halves make a perfect whole!" The prayer is indissoluble.

Alas I never married, but I took my thrice beloved there in hope that she and I might be joined. Often India is in my thoughts. My work involves the three Abrahamic religions. But in my heart a goddess created the world: the female creatrix. My life in a sense has been a failure. Power and influence escape me and I have no relationship with a lady.

CHAPTER TWO

My secretary, known as One Star, rang me. He sounded worried.

'What is it One Star?'

'The boss is up in arms. I have a problem,' he added. 'The Wing Commander and his new wife have been held up. I fetched their daughters from school. The girls are upset and want to know when daddy will get home. It could be hours.'

'What can I do to help?'

'Perhaps come down here? Calm things down? Tell them a story while I get a handle on the parents' whereabouts.'

'Give me half an hour,' I said. 'The Ruler won't keep me for more than twenty minutes. Trust me.'

The Ruler was doing his "I am the Ruler" thing.

'I want to see more arrests,' he said, putting on his reading glasses. He looked at me over the top of them.

'These people with temporary visas are eating me out of house and home. That includes your secretary. I want him weeded out.'

'He is my PA.'

'You PA him too much. These people should only get the peanuts they make back home, no more.'

I can't disagree with him. The Ruler and I are old school.

'Your job is to bag the malcontents,' he went on. 'Parasites and conspirators. Throw them out.'

'You are lucky to have someone incorruptible like me.'

'Don't talk to me like that. You think you were hired to be my master? Your kind of probity is too expensive. There was a boy at my prep school, a Russian, I think. He made the other boys his slaves. His favourite was one called Ego, if I remember. I learned a lot from him.'

'I did not know you were at prep school.'

'My boys prefer America. I tell them how the British treated me. Anyway, arrest some miscreants immediately or I will replace you with an American.'

'These are unusual times,' he said, which as it happens is One Star's favourite dictum.

Ten minutes later I met two tear-stained girls, one about twelve the other maybe eight.

'Hang on,' said One Star. 'I've asked this gentleman to hold the fort while I fetch your parents. He's a good egg.'

This was greeted with nervous smiles.

'OK. Here's the play. I'm going to tell a story. Later I want you to think of a story of your own and tell it him. Off your own bat.'

Giggles met this idea. We were sitting on a large sofa which One Star had bought on offer at a store next to the mosque. The store had enormous windows through which you can see endless furniture. Such a nice idea. Bedu fitting out their tents with execrable Western designs. No style.

Their feet dangling above the linoleum floor, the girls looked at us expectantly. I have no idea what children want to hear about. In my narrow sphere, betrayal and revenge are favourite.

One Star kicked off. 'I'm going to tell you a tale,' he said, 'then one of you will follow.'

'Will we be killed?'

'Perhaps.'

The younger girl sighs and raises her eyebrows, then starts to cry.

'We run out of tales, and die, like?' said the twelve year old.

'Why is your sister crying?'

'She doesn't want to die. When will mummy and daddy be back? Shortly. Alright. I'll tell you a tale of betrayal.'

'Oh good,' they said.

'My tale is about a Vizier. A king has a Vizier. You know? Vizier?'

'A motorcyclist?' said the youngest one.

'A Vizier is like the head of the Civil Service, like,' said the older one.

'OK, Sacha. The Vizier offers to spend the night with the king and tell a story. This is the Vizier's story.

'There is a Queen. Her house is gold, her gravel chrysolite, rubies, pearls. The porch is made of jasper. They had money. Big time. She divorces the king. She dresses her daughter in beautiful tweeds, and silks, and pearls, and at parties brings her forth like the full moon on a starlit night.

'Like a sort of young Barbara Cartland?' I suggested.

'Who?' said the girls.

'They live together in a palace,' continued One Star, 'but the daughter decides to marry. She interviews men. She chooses the youngest.

'There is a fly in the ointment. The Queen is a narcissist and does not like her daughter's choice. The Princess arranges for him to be vetted by old men; she makes him accompany her ma to Wimbledon; you've heard of Wimbledon? He drinks scotch at 10.30 am. Stupid, really.'

At this stage it occurred to me that One Star was recounting a potted history gleaned from my personal confessions.

One Star decided to gee things up by pretending to play the young man. 'I was banished to Scotland,' he exclaimed histrionically. The one time I get down south for a weekend, I ask to see you. Oh no. It's Mummy and I have an engagement. So you don't love me after all?

'Calm down,' squeaks One Star in a girl's voice. Deranged is so unattractive.

'So it's all over between us?'

'No point in continuing,' squeaks One Star indignantly.

'You're testing love to death.'

'No more Mr Nice Guy then!'

'Right then!'

'He put the phone down,' said One Star, 'and never saw her again.'

The younger girl starts to cry again. The older one winks.

'Later the Princess married a rich man who was an ifrit and a ghoul with lips like the kidneys of a camel,' said One Star. 'The lesson, girls, is avoid men seeking domination. I'm off to fetch your parents now. This gentleman is taking over.'

So I took over, saddened by One Star's tale. I sometimes wonder about him and why he is fascinated by conspiracy. The lesson, I told the girls, is that true love is selfless. 'What's the matter Sacha?'

She was crying now.

'The story was so sad,' she said. But the younger girl was beaming.

Well at least one of them got the message, I thought. Materialism, although a cliché, is a pathway to romance.

One Star can be impertinent.

'The Ruler thinks we're fiddling our expenses,' he said.

'Such prejudice is not uncommon,' I replied.

'I've been reading your private papers, sir,' he says. 'You spend too much time promoting America.'

'They are on our side, One Star, the side of freedom.'

'Tell that to the Shias, sir. Americans make a hash of the Middle East. They use Saudis as bait for Israel, and a counterweight to Iran. But the Chinese will bring Saudi and Iran together. Anyway Vietnam, Afghanistan and Iraq prove there are two sides to every freedom.

'Biden,' I replied, 'means *both* in German, that is to say, both English and Irish, slaver and enslaved, colonised and colonialist, sage and senile. That's diplomacy.'

'You mean that's America. A house that is divided cannot stand, sir.'

'America is not simple, One Star.'

'They want to foist their brand of democracy upon the world.'

'The Yanks won the Cold War. They keep the beacon shining.'

'Communism is not dead, sir. It is new and improved. I did a briefing note. Remember? Latin America has commies in their unions, and Judiciary. The Silk Road helps the Chinese to open another front. Russia and China are beavering together in the Arctic and Africa.'

'At the heart of China is the excellent Chinese Communist Party,' I said.

'That's it,' he said. 'The CCP are the only real democracy going, providing everyone is communist.'

'Well, the Chinese are doing great, building 50 ports in Africa and dams. They're spending a fortune, much of it borrowed.'

'What is remarkable is Chinese *long-term* thinking, sir. I just question the Pax Americana. I have heard men say the Americans are congenitally divided and short term. By having one Party the Chinese are unified, long term, and, in their way, the natural champions of Peace, providing their sphere of influence is properly negotiated. Americans have war written in their DNA. Their war of independence was a Civil War between you Britons.'

'No, it wasn't.'

'The Americans were treasonable, siding with the French. They refused to pay for an army, which defended them. Greed was at the heart of it. Trump mixes up greed and great. He harks back to when Americans dispensed with loyalty, mobbing and killing those who defended them. That's betrayal.'

'There's all kinds of democracy, One Star. America's is best.'

'Americans and Frenchies mistrust Government. Both revolutions killed a lot of people, sir. Both invented poor constitutions. Both have incoherent demographics.'

'How do you mean?' 'It's about power. Who has it? And what for? In America it was a beanfeast for the ruling classes. Poverty, expropriation of land and huge capital projects, all very profitable. Democracy and its demos are about *unity.* That's why it was invented. In America there is little democracy. To enter the Second World War the Japanese and the Germans had to declare war on America to get them to join in. The President facing an election did not want to squander German votes.'

'How does that work?'

'Their constitution, party politics, and above all *ethnic* divisions defy purpose. Chaotic immigration defies togetherness. There are multiple cultures in America. Many remain half asleep because their passions fall outside the system. The USA is so big, its politics is to do scale. Why did they invent Presidents? To have a bigger, better George III? No, they have cynical old men, stooges, and enormous funds. Corruption is inevitable. And only two parties, which hate each other. Debates about trivia like identity are displacement activities.'

'It is a well-oiled system that serves them well.'

'Communism is their bugaboo to the point of hatred. We Indians permit communism. Look at Kerala. We're grown up.'

'I don't understand you. Hate is passionate confrontation and should be encouraged. A bit more hate could have stopped Hitler.'

'If you have two parties that do not talk to one another, let alone agree, bureaucracy takes over, sir, a deep bureaucratic state within the state. We Indians know all about that.'

'How so, One Star?'

'Civil servants working out of sight to an undemocratic agenda.'

'Democracy works,' I replied. 'It took the American revolution to blow off the doors of history. America dragged us all into the light of day.'

'American democracy is anarchy. Do you not see, sir? Two parties knocking ten bells off each other, for short term gain. They are paid to disagree and lie professionally, their politics based on cannon fodder, sweated labour, refugees, no socialism. That says it all.'

'America is our paymaster.'

'America is plutocratic. Britain is plutocratic without the wealth. Both are racist, sir.'

'No, we're not.'

'Indians reinvented cricket and made it profitable. The Brits think cricketers hate immigrants. *That* is racism. In India we saved cricket. We rescued your car industry too.'

'Much as I love India, you exaggerate,' I said.

'All I'm saying sir is that your Americans are imperialists and bloody. They don't need you to spy for them.'

'You Indians are late arrivals at the party.'

'We have hope, we have purpose; we breed. America, Germany do not breed. They import people. In the Middle East, in Yugoslavia, in Southeast Asia, and now Ukraine, America imagines they are sorting out lesser men, undemocratic men, barbarians. They dismantle empires but do nothing for the survivors. Remember Mobutu? And now Islamists are taking over West Africa. To promote their so-called democracy, America *prevents* reconciliation, which is the absolute precondition to saving the planet.'

'Oh that! What has that to do with anything?' I said crossly.

'Their elite are always on the make. Guns, exploiting immigrants, sexism, corruption, political violence, are their way of life. Equality was a lie. Americans capitalism is based on *inequality*. If you cannot treat your own people equally you will never treat other countries as equal. The consequences are enormous.'

'They are the paymasters.'

'You've spent your life trying to get Arabs interested in democracy. But some don't like it. Religion, sexism and obedience get in the way. The joke is on America, which is not a democracy at all. It is an ethnocracy. It imported cheap labour without principle. Scale and profit were everything. In its DNA is exploitation, slavery, and the pork barrel. From what I've read violence was a way of life for British immigrants, from the borders, from the Highlands, and from Ireland. These traits were exploited by succeeding waves of capitalists. The results are stunning if you get rich. But the British industrial revolution taught squalor, misery, injury, death. The Americans went further. From the outset their greed was sharper. They went fishing in Ireland, Russia, Italy, South America, even China. Capital like a wolf greedily followed the weak and needy immigrant.'

'It's called the modern world,' I said.

'The Jewish lobby promotes its interests as the interests of America. Israel behaves as an American colony. Both America and Israel are founded on the settler mentality. Annexation of land, creeping, unremitting annexation, illegal, immoral, inhumane. America's so called democracy was similarly shaped by swarms of settlers seizing land, and monetising greed. A capitalism emerged stripped of humanity. Israel learned from its master. It is funded unconditionally, as an American weapon of choice. When Israel oversteps the mark, the American Government pretends innocence. That is what I call the ethnocratic system.'

'Whatever you call it, it works.'

'Bin Laden and Khalid Sheikh Mohammed revealed, in extreme form the hatred of US policies which favour Israel. Moderates in the region hid their rage. American narcissism allowed continuous settlements by a defiant Israel.'

'It's more complicated than that,' I said.

'America thinks Saudi and Israel will serve America's purpose. But Saudi, which is no friend to the West, demands equality with Israel in military technology, while collaborating with Russia in OPEC and decoupling oil sales from petrodollars.'

'Ethnic lobbying, deal making and violence undermine American democracy in other ways, One Star continued. Noraid funded terror in Ireland while America pretended otherwise. That was not democratic. No it was ethnocracy at work.'

'How many Mexicans are there in the USA, sir? Forty million? What is changing America? Death by Fentanyl. By the time China and India declare war on each other, the US will have imported enough Chinese and enough Indians to re-enact their war in prime time in America. Look at American genocide and massacres in the past: not least of Puerto Ricans, of indigenous people and of blacks. The original Homestead Act made violence American, democratic, inadmissible, ineradicable.

'What would you have us do? Shouldn't you be back at work?'

'What can we do? Get real. Be honest. *Respect* ethnic differences. How else will the world unite?'

'Sorry, old boy our job is to spy on the Iranians. Have you done that paper for me on Iranian drones?'

'Our job, according to you sir, is to get Iran in our sights and deliver them to our masters. I'm on the case.'

'I don't understand you. America painstakingly and openly promotes liberal values. You and I successfully isolate the enemy, watch them, and get into their heads. Have you got anything better to do?'

'I understand.'

'You're not yet 40, One Star, so your youth excuses this hysteria. But our game is to make America great again.'

'My game,' he replied, is to save the planet. Wouldn't it be great if the Americans rewrote their constitution?'

The Ruler is right, I thought. *It's time One Star was sent home.*

'Don't fiddle your expenses,' was my parting shot.

I have to admit my support for America is taking a bit of a knock.

CHAPTER THREE

My ex- girl friend Amelia studies the immune system and among other things, parasites. I hate her but she is often right.

Half the people on Earth she says, are infected with parasites. The immune system keeps much of this in check. When women get infected during pregnancy they pass parasites on to the unborn child. Toxoplasma gondii infects most warm-blooded animals, including humans. Its host in which genetic exchange occurs, is cats. In England every other person has a cat. An infected cat can crap up to 500 million toxoplasma oocysts in two weeks. Even one oocyst is infectious.

'This is Nature at work,' said Amelia. 'One consequence is that mice are manipulated to stop fearing cats. The parasite wants the mice to get up close and personal with the cats to download the parasite. For example, the infection causes wolves to shadow big cats like cougars. They ingest cougar poo. Humans can also be infected. Schizophrenia may follow. It happens that the current mental health problem is partly due to brain disease.' That's what Amelia told me and she's a scientist. She made a study of it.

It is not widely known but Stalin lived in the remote hamlet of Kareika, in the province of Yeniseisk. He had a cat and used to hunt, and fish in his spare time, Kareika being on the banks of a river of the same name. Stalin had a room in a peasant's hut and lived a peasant's existence. In the tundra round there fish abounded in the river, and the land teemed with wildlife now near extinct. He killed a leopard.

Stalin contracted an infection which stayed with him right up until his death. The effects are yet to be fully understood. Some say he became dogmatic, lost confidence; got jealous, secretive, yet also in a way entrepreneurial. His lack of conscientiousness was noted by Kruschev.

Stalin courted danger, and arguably was aggressive, and sanctimonious for example in his interpretations of Marx. But he was not alone in this.

Businessmen do not hold economists in high regard. They make economic predictions of their own. Many are unable to understand how economists took Marx seriously, let alone his ideas on dictatorship. Not all businessmen are wedded to equality as a driving force in human evolution or even as an interesting idea. Some are baffled by the acceptance of equality by the political classes. Proletariats fail to make good dictators. Proletariats are dire. Peasants are systematically killed by them. Gandhi did not approve.

From this I developed a theory that Marxists, starting with Lenin, were unwitting hosts to T Gondii and their witless behaviour had simple causes. However I have to widen this theory to include businessmen. In the Behemoths of business you would be surprised how many CEOs actually see themselves as alpha. Since the companies they dominate are often largely male, they frighten and oppress male underlings, who strangely find this reassuring. They value stability above bravery.

Now I know that peering into people's heads is considered politically incorrect. But it is self evident that I have to investigate the unAmerican activities of Iran if we are to reveal their deeper needs. A very small study in Denmark (151 people). showed respondents exposed to T Gondii ending up with schizophrenia. When the researchers looked at the timing issue— they found these individuals were 2.5 times more likely to develop the disease post-exposure. Stalin falls into this category. Chief execs of multinationals also.

There are still many who admire Stalin, not least the Turkic Soviets. He was respected for the vast projects he directed.

Like Tolstoy he saw Government as corrupt. Unlike Tolstoy he favoured autocratic rule. Julius Caesar was an early proponent of genocide. His genocide may have been due to abnormalities in his brain. Stalin's aggression drew him to Government.

Testosterone was a factor in his quest for power, which, once attained, he fiercely clung to by destabilising the structures and personnel supposedly in place to help him. This instability made him irreplaceable.

You may say this is story telling. But wait a minute. Consider the races of tyrants in the past. Let us classify tyrants as a race, let us judge them as such. Prejudice, accurately deployed, can save lives. Tyrants who survive, are very odd. Like Nebuchadnezzar, Stalin moved populations about when he was not killing Tatars. In evolutionary terms is it not possible that despots share similar traits which favour their genomes' survival? Much evolution is built on symbiosis, some on parasitism. These tyrants carry in their biome mysterious forces that fit them for the enormous task of dictatorship. It is my job to check Iran's leadership against appropriate criteria.

The human brain is the favourite diet of a number of parasites ranging from rabies, trypanasomiasisa, to the amoeba naegleri fowleri which feasts on the human brain.

I regularly have nightmares in which parasites are proliferating in me.

Gut microbiota, Amelia once said, include parasites that have a role in Alzheimer's and Parkinson's.

Adult humans harbour 200 to 300 different bacterial species, most in the ileum and colon. Like the Irish, and many nascent nationalities they have been part of a larger life form, but have left it and gone their own way. Americans decided long ago to support such revolutions. Tell that to the Congo. America hasn't even begun to think through the consequences. My job is to help them.

The human genome contains about 23,000 genes but gut microbiota provides up to 10 million genes and about 600,000 per person. Darwin argued that extinction is a necessary part of evolution. Extinction is now out of control. It is humans – call it their free will – that are destroying the Earth. Potentially, microbiota are small atom bombs.

So, it pays to entertain blue sky thoughts about parasites. Do they infest dictators? Do they by evolution transform clades? Species? With our blessing do they have their own version of evolution with no end in sight, no destination, no purpose, save for the churning of extinction and morphologies which are hastening the planet's demise.

We can defend ourselves by self-sacrifice, self-pruning, self pollarding. Can this be done unilaterally? No. We must create a pax panica, to save Nature from humans. One Star is insistent on this point. The evidence is growing that oil majors and governments are backsliding on the measures needed to cap global warming. We need obedience, and probity, ubiquitous and aligned, if necessary enforced.

Let us consider the role of tyrants who specialise in human obedience.

You only have to study Sicilian history to find humans, both democrats and tyrants, endlessly knocking ten bells out of each other. You may counter this by suggesting reincarnation as an explanation for the recurrence of tyrants. This does not diminish the idea of tyranny as a violent male incubus, which appears throughout history, intent on acts of destruction not least on females and submissive victims.

Poor Stalin. Fear of failure and a monstrous appetite to subdue others, were caused by a parasite. Let us imagine T Gondii, dormant, sitting in the brain and at the back of the eye. It hides and replicates slowly, bestially. The consequences in mice are behavioural changes such as failure to groom, loss of balance, and diminished strength. Stalin groomed his moustache to offset smallpox scars, and as a gesture to insult Lenin. We can't say what came first: the infection or the trait. I reflect on Stalin, on Mao. Which was madder? I fall back on the role of disease and medicine in those who crave to be leaders.

Of course scientists deny Stalin had parasites; historians deny Marx was mad. The media continuously rewrite history to sell copy. But the point of social media is to put newspapers out of business and drive a stake through the hearts of fascists and communists in the media and put an end to their sticky necrophilia. Each side competes by claiming their adversaries murdered more victims, some even pretending that the mad King of the Belgians had an ideology of mutilation that makes Stalin palatable. To this I ask in all innocence: What is the difference between Bush junior and Leopold (or even Blair)? None of them spent time in the jurisdictions where they enacted their ignorance. Increasingly parasites are discovered to manipulate their hosts. Microbes in the gut influence human diets. Fungi make ants climb trees and pour spore out of their heads. Others inject psilocybin or a khat equivalent into hosts to make them trip and do their bidding. Hair worms make mantises and crickets drown themselves in order for the parasites to reproduce.

If this seems unnatural think of Hitler. He engineered his people to expect endless war. Those who accepted not just privation, but mass deaths included the very young and the very old. But it seems absolute war was not just Hitler's idea but that of many others. Like mantises and crickets, people committed suicide often pro patria.

This behaviour looks alarmingly like manipulation by parasites. Is it not possible that war, ever with us, is a disease, or at least the product of one? It is no use pretending Hitler was a nightmare, or a metaphor. He was a person, an extraordinary human being. The Americans taught their young after the war that the German problem was economic, not moral. The German people had endured such economic stress that they turned to Hitler and to war, or so Americans argued. This conveniently makes Hitler a bad choice, but an intelligible one, since hungry and cold people were in a state of trauma. But at the end of the war the German people suffered trauma in their defeat at the hands of the Russians. Yet they recovered extraordinarily quickly to resume democracy and morality, as if they had just been temporarily off sick. After all they had introduced universal suffrage well before Britain. They had the toolbox and great resilience to survive and prosper. But many of them did love Hitler and militarism and did not rate democracy much on the evidence of its contribution to their history. For this reason, their democracy proved ephemeral. What is so worrying is that Hitler and millions of his followers existed at all.

I view Hitler as a nightmare, from which I wake in terror, often under the impression that he is in my bedroom.

Marxists hate Gandhi for depriving them of violence. They pretend to like Tolstoy, despite his Christian anarchism. Some believe the problems of mid-twentieth century Europe were the confrontation between communism, and national socialism which had a great deal in common. Hitler and Stalin and their followers were infected with parasites. Gandhi rose above hatred. He included Islam in his idea of India, despite history.

In a café off the Edgeware Road, I fell into conversation with this Indian guy about Freddie Mercury, who was a Gujerati. Freddie was born in Zanzibar and from there lived in numerous places which invariably ruled homosexuality unlawful.

'He became an anarchist like Gandhi,' said the Indian guy proudly.

'Was Gandhi a Gujerati too.'

'Absolutely. He was also very taken by Tolstoy.'

'Another Gujerati?'

'No! Tolstoy was Russian, the most famous Russian ever.'

'Are you a Gujerati?'

'I am part of a world in which peace and love and profit coexist.'

'Were you ever in the Gulf?' I asked.

'Yes, but mainly Uganda and Dar as Salaam, a bit like Freddie.'

'I hear the food is wonderful.

'Yes', he said, taking out a business card.

'The future is in the Gulf,' he said, and gave it me.

'But the Gulf is arid and infertile and presumably will get worse?'

'It might,' he said.

'Even the Zagros Mountains are degraded,' I replied. 'Biodiversity is under threat everywhere.'

'The Muslim world has ambitions in Africa.'

'You mean Saudi?' I asked. 'So do the Russians. They should get together.'

'They have,' he said.

'The Gulf is torn between Saudi and Iran, isn't it?' he continued, 'each separated by tectonic plates, isn't it? India,' he said, 'has always been aligned with Russia, the old Tolstoy Gandhi axis. More scientific than Islam, more spiritual and socialist than the West, India is the future.'

'The USA controls the Gulf and keeps Saudi and Iran in order,' I ventured.

My career started then. I took the American shilling.

So, in that café off the Edgeware Road my future was launched. Full of smoke as caffs were in them days, it hummed with conversation.

'Are you a Muslim? Or a Hindoo?' I asked. 'I'm a Gujerati, one hundred percent,' he said. 'We are truly an international tribe.' Sucking deeply on a cigarette, back in the day, his smooth handsome face shone, and his quinquevalent fingers seemed to sip and taste the smoke, like hummingbirds.

'I am sent here and there by the job centre', said a short man at the next table, dressed, inappropriately, it seemed back then, in a dishdasha.

'You a Muslim? I can tell,' I said percipiently.

'I am of course,' he said. 'Nature is made by God. Western science is subject to God's wishes,' and he twitched at his dishdasha below the table. We translated Aristotle and, so as not to offend God, we improved it. Medicine, mathematics, and astronomy,' he said modestly, were upgraded. 'As for creation and biodiversity we invented them with divine guidance.'

I found this eminently reasonable. But the Gujerati replied with energy.

'All humanity stands accused, of harming life of greed and of trivialising nature, of narcissism, of fixating on identities while the world burns. What are you doing about it?'

'We apply ourselves,' replied the chap in the dishdasha. 'This is life,' he said. *He might be a Zanzibari,* I thought. 'We live for many different reasons,' he continued. 'We do what we can. Sometimes we do nothing. But this is life. Neither we nor our enemies live for no reason. We choose this path, then another one. We must proceed. If we offend it is because things lose shape and balance and we have to change direction, often at short notice. But we have the book. Neither we nor our enemies deliberately harm nature. We are engaged in complex activities, powerful needs, drives, emotions. We are put here to worship God. On all sides we are constrained by legacies, and rules, and are not certain what will happen, in a minute, an hour, in a lifetime. This life is about worshipping God. Only sometimes is it about defeating an enemy. A greater part is perfecting ourselves for submission and prayer. Where does nature fit in? In truth nowhere, save as God's protectorate, delegated to believers, to take care of.'

This sounded truthful and reasonable. 'There you are then,' I said. But I could see a pattern. The Americans were leading their clients in a manoeuvre against Russia and against China. Persia has long been susceptible to Russian influence. Russia was suspicious of Mossadegh yet was steadfast and determined to support the Iranian revolution. Britain tried to stop Russia interfering in the region. America, inclined to put their chosen men in power, dismantled British imperialism by forging their own. A bit like driving a car without a lesson. Saudi are pouring money in to advance their version of religion. China wants to pre-empt America in the Gulf.

My career choice is clear. The world was on a knife edge. Global warming is life threatening. Countries may have to coerce vast numbers to save nature. We must hold their feet to the fire. They must respect the West and its science.

Is there any chance this will succeed? We must try. America, according to One Star cannot be trusted to tailor their imperium dispassionately. Europeans, by serving America, must control her. Let us disentangle her from her rivalries but stand four square with her in the Middle East. Then, I thought, *that sounds silly.*

If Russia sees Iran as a strategic partner against the West, we must prevent this. Iran and Russia have a long-standing attachment. Both hoped for a certain kind of India. When America and China agree a Modus Vivendi the Gulf will also have to choose. Saudi, possibly UAE, will choose America if only to weaken Iran.

'No,' I said. 'that will never do. America cannot put Israel and Saudi in the same bag. It is unnatural.'

I personally have become obedient to a Gulf ruler, but I am watchful, protective and ever loyal to America's values despite her hypocrisy. Little does One Star know my career was launched by a Gujerati.

I have a fond memory of that old fellow spinning me his yarns.

The Gujeratis are the greatest race on earth, he claimed. 'Bapa Gandhi, Jinnah Chandaria, Nusserwanji Tata, Modi, all gujjus,' he said spinning his plate around in elliptical shapes, adding expression, charm, and ambiguity to his conversation. Everyone knows Gujeratis are famous for business. But this old guy's claims were wide ranging.

'I believe indigenous people watch and protect biodiversity,' he explained. 'That's how important they are. Gujeratis know this. Planet Earth must retain the boreal forests and peat lands across Russia, China and the US. That's how much they have in common.'

At Cop27, Brazil, the DRC and Indonesia announced the big three rainforest coalition. They said they would coordinate talks on their conservation. The Brazilian president said he would convene a pan-Amazonian meeting on its conservation. Indigenous groups propose a protected area to cover the world's largest rainforests, equivalent to the size of Mexico, to be created and to be known as 80 by 2.

But in the café on Edgeware Road this ambition was not evident. Gujerat, the man said, is the font of civilisation. Only us Indians can save the world. Only Gujerat can save India.

I saw then that everywhere man is a plague. They consume animals, vegetation and all the minerals of the Earth. The plague has entered a new phase and infects more and more regions. What will happen as the plague unfolds?

'Tell me,' I said to the Gujerati, 'where you come from, is it utterly consumed and a kind of waste?' 'Not at all. If that is what you want, then go to the Middle East. Much of the place is barren save for alfa alfa grass and date palms and not much grows that has not been paid for by the West in petrodollars.'

'Why is it in poor condition?' I asked. 'Is it squandered and mishandled?'

'Not exactly. In the coastal areas there is a sort of farming which drilled too many wells until the water table was ruined and salinity became pervasive. Did you know that by extracting water mankind seriously disturbs the planet itself? In the interior the Bedu live traditional lives, harsh and introverted, with little to enable them to retrieve the green world that once existed there thousands of years past. The world's resources must be much better protected by Gulf rulers.'

'Then I will visit the Gulf.'

'If you want to see biodiversity, first go to India. Remember only this: your fine plans will lead nowhere unless you love and worship. So I did. I took Amelia to India. We found enough sects and customs, behaviours and beliefs, to glimpse biodiversity in a new way, also many on the margin of starvation and of death.

My future was cast there and then. I immersed myself into Gulf politics. I made my number with the Americans. They set out to tie Iran in knots. They needed a point man. Iranian theocrats destabilise the Gulf and Iraq, they said. We wish to stop this.

I placed myself at the heart of it. I am that point man. But all those years ago I found, time and again, the Iranians to be as resourceful and just as idealistic as their enemies. I will risk my neck.

My secretary, One Star, a Gujerati, brought bad news.

'Sir,' he said, 'your friend Toby from Oxford has been on. He sends bad news I am afraid. The great love of your life Amelia Pageant is heading this way. Do we need to inform the Directorate, sir?'

'What's it got to do with them? That is private.'

'No, sir. Nothing is private. You are as subject to the Official Secrets Act as I am. Should we notify the Ruler?'

'Damn it, One Star, no! Anyway, how on earth do I endanger you?'

'You could be working for the opposition, sir?'

'They are too intelligent to employ me. Anyway, which opposition?'

'Existentially speaking sir, everyone is opposition. Mr Maniwal was beguiling me over coffee yesterday. He says that on the grapevine you are known as St John Philby 'minor' because of your propensities. He says you are known to be a triple agent. Can that be good for business?'

'I'm not a triple agent. OK One Star. Leave it with me.'

'Just one other thing, sir.'

'Yes, yes, One Star?'

'Toby arrives at midnight. Will he be staying at your place?'

'Have him met and delivered, please. Oh, and send in Mrs Goldiwallah.'

'Yes sir, but in 40 minutes your Iranian marker is calling in.'

I was having an affair with this Mrs Goldiwallah, entirely in the line of duty. Her husband is involved in a scam to wrest control of liquor distribution away from the established channels. He has set up a company offshore to this end. My plan is to exchange favours and confidences with her, sufficient to expose him.

'Good morning. Mrs Goldiwallah,' I greeted her.

'Good morning, sir.' And she smiled a charming, raffish, smile, though her unusual dentistry rather glittered.

'Mrs Goldiwallah, you are very welcome for reasons I need not divulge; walls have ears. May we get down to business?'

'Of course. Which business would that be? she raffishly smiled again.

'No not that sort. Please read back to me the first two pages of my autobiography.'

'Yes sir,' and at this she laughed girlishly.

She cleared her throat.

'I will work in the Middle East,' she recited, 'as long as I can worm my way into every segment of expatriate and indigenous life, revolutionary, capitalist, Islamist. Alright so far, sir?'

She went on: 'I am a supporter of a school building pro-gramme. I give lessons on local culture and religion. As a result, two girls came to my attention. Both beautiful, though naturally off limits they reminded me of Amelia Pageant.'

'Is this confession wise, sir?'

'Maybe not.'

She continued: The real me is inconspicuous. It is perfectly all right to admit working for the Research Department; which, as everyone knows, reports to the Ruler. Most people think it is the Statistics office, and I do nothing to disabuse them. In reality I am engaged in sophisticated surveillance, including the arrest, and expulsion (or worse) of political malcontents.'

'Beautifully phrased, sir,' said Mrs Goldiwallah, simpering.

'Thank you, Mrs Goldiwallah.'

'In the Gulf things are done differently, she recited. 'For one thing there is the great rift in religious beliefs that arose in the dawn of time, and now seems so deep a once great culture is in danger of being torn asunder. Whichever side you are on, you blaspheme.'

'Our neighbour across the straits, a sovereign state, occupies a position clear cut and adversarial. Intelligent and cultured, it is well versed in democracy, but gives precedence to religion, and occasional violence. It is good at plots, espionage and counter espionage. Its interests, among other things. include championing populations repressed by the other side. I am barred from going there. Across the straits that is.'

'Are you really?' asked Mrs Goldiwallah.

'Not invariably.'

'Our other neighbours are neither attractive nor tractable. Everyone is engaged in the Yemen, one way or another. And then to the south there is Africa, a source of wealth, gold, and slaves. Once an empire stretching to the great mosque of Djenne, it now lies teeming, and helpless as birds of prey circle. May I suggest we excise that bit?

'But why? We'll talk about this outside the office,' I said smiling coyly.

'As you wish. Shall I continue?'

'Yes, please. Better to discuss private matters in privacy.'

'All of these issues fall across my desk,' she continued as she read her shorthand. 'I am a natural candidate for accusation, conspiracy, plots, betrayal. Yet I seem to get along. The retreating tide of empire left behind a surprising ecosystem Experts, political, military, economic, legal to name but a few. I cultivate them, in small ways. I enjoy the confidence of rulers on both sides. Embassies open their doors to me.

'Do I enjoy this life? The sensory side is delightful, the weather crap. Is it leading anywhere? There is always that risk. Does it satisfy my personal ambitions? No. Is it socially adjacent? Absolutely not. The longer I stay the more supercilious and isolated I become. So few locals come from the top drawer, and befriend me. Of the expatriates none would get into my golf club back home. Nearly all are guilty of cupidity. What is worse they pretend professionally and socially to be what they are not. A lawyer here is unlikely to be accepted as a partner in a UK practice. A managing director here has usually never managed anything back home. A banker is, often as not, on the run from some enquiry. All scratch backs and rub along nicely.'

'So how do I get by? I retreat into myself. I sail a bit. I paint, I study the history and archaeology of the region. I read poetry.

I make no friends until, that is, events require otherwise.'

She wriggled a bit, gave a hearty sigh and departed, and Esa, my opposite number, came by. 'Quick One Star. Where's my briefing notes?'

'Here, sir.' He hands me a file.

'That should be a single piece of paper,' I say officiously.

In comes Esa. I greet him. 'How good to see you, Esa.'

'Salaam Aleikum el Hamdulillah. Kaif Halak? Boss!'

'So what's up, Esa? You well?'

'Always.'

'I've got this file here from One Star about the build up. I'll skip the stuff about combat ready marines, blah. aircraft in Kuwait, warplanes in Bahrein blah, innumerable drones.

'Let me see now. US battle groups. I remember the good old George Washington. And USS Independence. Now things keep changing I get confused. But we have an aircraft carrier nearby. Better fighters; millions more pounds of ordinance; missiles, laser guided bombs, general purpose bombs, bombs… bombs. Thank God for America. But what have you got? Don't pretend you know. You change your minds more frequently than your underwear.

I lick my fingers.

Cruisers, tomahawk capable, numerous destroyers, guided missile frigates, attack submarines. Then I realise, One Star has given me the old file, now out of date. Oops.

'Now you must get out of the Red Sea,' I admonish him. 'The Houthis are in your debt? They're a nuisance. If there's going to be a naval battle what naval kit do you guys have now? What have you bought recently?' I said sternly. 'Exactly!'

'We make the best kit now. We have broken into the big time as armaments manufacturers. We even sell stuff to the French. Why do they have a base here? The Brits used to have Maktoum's back.'

'French restaurants are a core industry,' I said. 'You eat Michelin in Paris?'

'I prefer steak and kidney.'

'Good man. Good man. Now what have you got?'

'We have ideas. America has no ideas. Nuclear bombs do not work in Afghanistan. North Korea and Pakistan give us missiles. For over thirty years now. And Russia. Very old allies. So watch out. Abu Dhabi buys from North Korea and we get commission. Don't we?'

'Do you now? You need the money. But the US owns the IMF.'

'Soon China will. They love our oil. We support human rights in Iraq, in Lebanon, in Yemen. Costs a lot. International community must pay. Trump cancelled first class diplomatic bridge we built around nuclear. China lends us funds to buy their very nice submarines. Two navies, a regular one and one IRGC. Very quick ships and what we call drones. Alireza Tangsiri ran up debts. Who gonna pay? We have secret ballistic missile. Expensive. And to help Houthis, we borrow from China.'

'And who are they borrowing from?' I jeered.

'Soon America gonna break up,' he said. 'Remember we are Europe's friends. We propose nuclear free zone. But Satan stopped all that.'

'Is that all you got? Really?'

He smiled. 'We have enough to pull the American nose down a peg. We have allies. Maybe soon a new big, big one. And we are now best manufacturer of drones in the world. We supply Ukraine, and Russia, North Korea and Pakistan. And France, in secret.'

'Your new ally sent a thousand junks to Ormuz? Called China? Eh?'

'Maybe. And where your little English aircraft carrier? Is it sunk? Oh dear.'

'You're stuck with second class stuff, now, aren't you?'

'I don't know. Honest. Have you seen our excellent kit for underwater use? And you my good friend. You must be busy with all the money laundering here, the gold smuggling, the empty properties? For you much work. Now tell me. This Ministry of Tolerance. What is it?'

'You know, Esa, I am on your side. Nobody likes Isis. You don't. We don't. So, we are all on the same side now, eh?'

'Better be, or as they say Hormuz will be a tide of blood. Ha!'

'Arabia had to kneel before the Ming. Can you guarantee protection?'

'You got someone important needs protecting? Just say the word. Esa see to it. We need to meet again next week. We are going to swoop.'

'Swoop?'

'Arrests. Swoop.'

'I have a lady scientist coming. But the advice is: Only go for essential travel. No dual nationals. Is it a sin to marry foreigners in your country?'

'I have distance learning module for you. You need a refresher. You can't airbrush out religion, you British.'

'Thanks. Look forward to it. Love you more than all the other girls.'

CHAPTER FOUR

That night Toby arrived perspiring unattractively, at two in the morning.

'Hello Toby,' I greeted him.

'Hello Dylan.'

'So what's all this about Amelia? I asked cheerfully.

'She was the most important thing ever to befall you.'

He was wrong. The least intelligent are always quick to give advice. I didn't like to say so but I heartily dislike Amelia. She is a scientist, a materialist, and neglects the spiritual and the aesthetic. How foolish is that? Like many feminists she thinks promiscuity a human right. Toby poor fellow is on her side. Many people have never even experienced a kiss. I bet whatever sex Toby has is loveless. I know he loves someone but has never had sex with them. Loveless sex and sexless love are pointless since they fail the test of stability. Amelia I loved briefly, but she refused sex.

My indifference towards Amelia is fundamental. She is a yes woman given over to scientific hyperbole. I cannot be doing with Darwin. He built a theory of evolution in which extinction is the engine of change. He gave no thought to the effect this would have on human behaviour. Humans have taken to extinction like ducks to water. Science merrily furnishes endless justifications to destroy Nature. They have below average ethics. To put it another way they bet on biology and physics the same way Wall Street bets on greed. Both demand freedoms which destroy lives. I do not think too highly of Amelia.

I am on the lookout for Love in small packages. A man who works at gentle empathy is more likely to love a wife and children. To put it another way if you're on the lookout for the love of your life (I do not mean the sex of your life) exercise empathy and you are at the races. One day you will get it right.

I think it was Tolstoy who said everyone thinks of changing the world, but no-one thinks of changing himself. This has something to do with it.

'Personally,' said Toby, 'I think Amelia was a gigantic cock up.'

'We had a falling out. She told me she couldn't have children,' I replied.

'As if you don't know, she's had two children. How many have you?'

'I am free. That's what matters.'

'It was a test obviously,' he said.

'Which she failed.'

'No, she was testing you.'

'If you love someone, you forgive them being selfish. But if you are *in love* with someone, it is different. In those circumstances you are caught in a storm. Control's impossible. You make passionate vows. If you break them, it spells disaster.'

'First I've heard of it. Is love a brain disease; is that what you mean?'

'Disease can sometimes make you happy, like bi-polar. Being in love is a slalom. Once you kick off you don't know what's next. Start a fire in the bedroom, chances are you can't control it.'

'From what I hear you're not on fire. Sounds like Amelia wasn't either. '

'Never confuse marriage with love. Never forget the insanity,' I growled.

'First I've heard of it,' he said again. 'In your case love is a brain disease. I'm certain of it.'

The next day we went into the desert to take a breath of parched air, and do a recce. I felt at the time an inclination to execute great landscapes.

It was early in the morning, a time in the peninsula of absolute magic, before the heat gets unbearable, when light enriches everything like an enamel, and huge horizons open before heat closes them down again.

Toby had something on his mind. He was not remotely interested in me or Amelia. He was, in a maudlin way, preoccupied with himself.

'I made a terrible mistake,' he said. 'I should have stayed in Denmark.'

I was not sure why the girl had not left Denmark herself. She insists he immigrate lock stock and barrel. I sought to tease this out.

But first I helped him, by recounting my own experiences.

'Amelia was crippled by her ma's ambitions. Ever hear anything so odd?'

'Mothers don't come into it.'

'Mothers take precedence. Amelia was jealous of my freedom. A virago, her idea was to behave just as she wanted. Like a man does. Her words not mine; she imagines that's how men behave.'

'Bullshit!' he said.

'Her mother laid down rules. Amelia never challenged Mummy and prolonged an infantile persona to keep things sweet. In short Mummy trained her to a sort of passivity. Narcissism.'

'That really doesn't sound like her.'

'I remember I felt another man must lie behind the problem. I sensed him in the shadows. Was she planning an independent future with him? But the thing that got to me was the materialism. It was the backbone of her scientific career. It made her even more subordinate to her mother. It ruled out religion, and all that is spiritual in art, even free will. Conversation was impossible.

'You look down on her with contempt, yet competed with her.'

'You have no idea. Passion was everything. Hunger, total abandon. In my case lust unfulfilled. She came to believe she was in love with me, but of course she wasn't. I was more experienced than her. I knew that she had affection for me, but not love as a young man needs it.'

'I've heard it all before,' Toby yawned. 'I have problems too.'

His self doubt has no value whatsoever.

'Now about this landscape,' I said, referring to a shapely dune, which in the middle distance, sat amidst a swell of little waves of scree. 'Where could we site the golden section?' I asked.

'Dunno,' said Toby. 'Would a camel do?'

Toby is not an artist.

'You forget,' said Toby, 'the desert is full of life, actually teeming with it, from spiders and wasps, to wolves and hyenas, and even leopards so I've read. You could make a golden section out of them?'

'That's nonsense. The survival of wild creatures round here is not even on the cards. To be fair the locals are friendly to the wild when it suits them. They hunt to kill.'

'What will you paint?' he asked. 'Where will you put your golden section?'

'There are ways,' I said, measuring as I went. 'Treat it as the sea.'

'What? Like Turner?'

I sucked my paintbrush. 'You know Turner had a place on his palette topped up with opium, which he sucked from the end of his brush. This explains his remarkable sense of colour. Yes, like Turner.'

'You mean he was a crack head?'

'All painters cultivated poison. Green, yellow, red, blue oils were all poisonous with arsenic, mercury, lead, or cadmium. Maybe that explains art, and why it kept changing. A painter like Turner used the same stuff they put on roads to dry paint; called gumtion. When he sucked his brush, he was ingesting sweet tasting white lead. Who knows, his love of yellow colour and his cataracts may just have been badges of honour. They all had diabetes in Turner's day. Lead could get you in the kidneys, or the heart. Turner had both plus he was a sherry head. But between bouts of depression he was happy.'

'So, let's pretend we are Turner. Let's lie in wait until a Simoom blows and shapes the desert into vast billowing clouds of silicate spray which the invading winds drive into our eyes, in painful mists and clouds, vortices of stone, shards and spears of light wounding and blinding us.'

Wow?

'Maybe painting was addictive. The chemistry changed his dopamine levels as well as his eyesight. I think it was like falling in love. Remember that, Toby? Falling in love? Diving into the unknown. Have you ever thought how this desiccation, all this dead matter has come to deform the poor devils in the interior?'

'No.'

'The tribes once knew this as a nascent paradise, fresh, green and wet, described by Enkidu, and called Dilmun. Their descendants have since become beetles, the black hooded variety, who scavenge the lifeless remains of this dead land. They live on nothing, produce nothing, survive on a diet of language, prayer, superstition and internecine strife. What has this place done for them?'

'No,' said Toby, smiling in his boyish way. 'You have often told me how gifted the inhabitants are: quick witted devoted to friends, prolific in love, the begetting of multifarious families and the multiplication of their genes. What turns you against them now? And in answer to your question, they have black shiny unctuous wealth, which they take out of the sand and then pour it back in. We then repaired to the bar of the latest golf club. 'Now tell me,' I said, 'how do you know Amelia is coming here? And why? She is a precious soul given to silks, and tweeds, and pearls, which will do very well in our air conditioning, but will she be socially satisfied?'

'What I hear,' said Toby, 'is she's gone severe and ascetic. You won't like it one bit. Not now. I was in my club, and someone mentioned the Flight Commander, Light, isn't he? Apparently, he's not a fit partner for any red-blooded woman.'

'Lightly you mean? She's not married to him anymore. Left him years ago. She is a top scientist in medicine. Works with a Professor, the man who is collaborating with her on some very strange stuff. I hear he's into opioids.'

'My God. He better not be or I'll sort him out.'

'You've been out in the Bundu too long.'

'Her ex-husband is here unbeknownst to her.'

'Anyway in my club they were full of it. Apparently, she knows the Ruler.'

'Who? Amelia? I doubt it. If she does I'd hear about it. I don't mix much with low brow expats here. My bag is archaeology, snake worship… Dilmun, the site of the Garden of Eden. Stuff like that.

'Garden of Eden near here? Well! Who would have thought it? You know you mustn't underestimate her. From what I hear she is intellectually turbo charged.'

I ask myself *what is her big brain for?* 'But, little Toby, the difference between us is I am free. She is not.'

'Come back to Blighty, where people matter.'

'British influence out here is on the wane. America is the game in town.'

'My dad always said greed and inequality feed off each other.'

A sermon was coming.

'Take racism,' he said. 'Who believes humans cannot interbreed? Who wants uncontrolled immigration? No-one. Yet politicians blackguard each other as racists. Then they break the iron rule of politics. They redefine the word racism to win the argument, so if you think about it the word now has no meaning whatsoever. Plus, the wrong sort of immigrants are portrayed as invaders, corrupting our way of life, of family, of morality. The other side accuse their opponents of bigging up ethnic minority votes. The politicians weaponise immigration, on this delusional battleground. The media make hatred their watchword in case they lose circulation. The FBI make things worse. The whole system is corrupt. The newly discovered bacillae of identity politics, and phoney rights lead to bureaucratic freeloading.'

'Thatcher's nonsense about the market determining growth only makes things worse,' I explained. 'After the war the industrial heritage of the Nazis was rescued by Americans who cut deals with German industrialists and scientists to make themselves great. In Italy the car workers sided with Agnelli, an ex-fascist, against the unions. You Brits went bust, Toby, by basking in the delusion of victory, prioritising the NHS for returning heroes. You actually helped German car makers get back on their feet. You should have snapped them up and employed them as Americans did in rocket science. Now British health is below Western standards you've just paid back your steepling NHS debts to America. Your management defeated Germans (they thought) then declared war on their own workers. Once Hamburg admired Manchester. Now Manchester envies Hamburg.'

'The answer,' said Toby 'is to abolish political parties. We need revolution *against* politicians. I once spent time in Rome's foremost hospital. A patient on admission was examined and every doctor in the vicinity formed his or her own diagnosis, all different. But then they thrashed out their differences and stuck to a single diagnosis. That is what politics needs. Unity.'

'My dear fellow,' I said condescendingly, 'come back down to earth or you'll be blackballed for such tosh. American democracy is the answer.'

Toby and I spent some time wind surfing. The sky was clear, and the climate unusually nice. Although the monsoon was in the offing. Toby had insisted we take a long yomp out to an oil tanker which from shore looked misty as a mirage and somewhat distant. It was a hell of a long way on a board, and this worried me as I didn't fancy being picked up by some Iranian cowboy. But everything went well.

I was glad to see him go. I had much too much to do to be acting as host to anyone and everyone who chooses to use my apartment.

All that chatter about Amelia had unmanned me. Toby is none too bright but his likening of love to a disease, is not without merit.

In my day I imagined love as a kind of conquest. I wanted Amelia to buy into my religion but as a narcissist she refused. My plan was to have children, and people Amelia with them forever. But then she chose to bear children for Wing Commander Lightly, God knows why.

I turned my mind to good works.

Asked to talk about colonialism to the children at the English Speaking School I put on a hair shirt. They must learn that the past fails the present. I chose some half-truths.

'Who colonised the Gulf?' I asked.

'We did,' they cried, inaccurately.

'You are at a crossroads here,' I said. 'There are places all round the world like this : The straits of Japan, the Channel, the Severoput passage, the Bosphorus, the Suez Canal, the straits of Taiwan, the Panama canal, and the Gulf. America keeps them open, a holy task. Even now America is helping keep the Red Sea open. So, originally a colony itself, it is reinventing freedom. People whinge about colonialism. America, starting as a colony, now bestrides the world. The Egyptians, the Phoenicians, the Chinese, the Greeks, the Romans pioneered colonies. Do not confuse colonies with conquest. To put it another way Roman conquest brought civilisation and the Pax Romana to Britain and the Middle East. But they killed masses of Celtic speaking people, which was a mistake. Failed genocide let in the Germans.

'American colonialism brings new life to others. Where are her enemies now? North Vietnam's sponsors have gone bust.

North Korea lives in poverty. Afghanistan reverts to patriarchy. The Greeks founded 500 colonies often as a destination for refugees fleeing famine, and death. Flight was amazingly popular then. Everyone was fleeing. Colonies were the safety valve. They saved millions of lives.

But the Greeks, masters of internecine violence, city versus city, created no Pax Hellenica, but enormous trade instead, like the good old UK. Great seafarers developed nations by trading with the locals.

'The word colonisation is used to describe oppression. Portugal, Spain, France, and Britain are seen as villains. Make no mistake: without profit, no civilised country would take the risk. Profit pays for what the State provides. Remember that next time you go to hospital.

'It is a shame the secrets of tribal societies for preserving Nature did not survive.

'The American revolution promoted democracy. The French revolution promoted massacre and oppression. France began with one little France at the centre, colonising neighbours like Brittany and Normandy make one single truly great country with Napoleon as Emperor whatever that meant.'

'Now that the developed world is failing to reproduce itself, expect reverse colonisation. Those once colonised replenish us by migrating here and lending us their sexual potency. Like birds or eels these people migrate uncannily to places whence their colonial masters set out, like Bristol. Just as our forebears fled famine, poverty, and hopelessness these latter-day immigrants come to us for the exact same reasons. Some are racist and sexual predators, of course. But the truth is the old colonies seeded these new reverse ones, in the midst of London, Paris, Birmingham. It was an idea as difficult to handle as a migrating eel.

I decided to lighten this dull topic. 'My favourite tipple,' I told the children, 'is wine. The Greeks colonised Marseilles. The Rhone valley benefitted (as did the Crimea) from colonial viticulture. If Gaul had not been colonised claret and burgundy would not exist. Brandy, a concentrate, was designed for long colonial voyages. There might never have been a Michelin without Tremalchio. The Romans made us civilised. Sadly they omitted Germany, Ireland, and Iran. In today's world there are hidden Chinese colonies throughout Asia and Africa. The Jewish diaspora spread enlightenment and art of extraordinary value all over the place. In Saudi the finest alcohol is available diplomatically. For too long the poorest expats had to do without baths, tuning bathrooms into distilleries and making poisons which pass for whisky, wine, whatever they command it to be, all made out of the exact same horrible liquid. Doing without baths in that climate, sacrifices fragrance for hooch.'

At this point a large sallow boy interrupted me.

'The point,' he said, 'is the old world colonised the new and got kilt.'

'Is this the Scottish Speaking School?' I asked, sarcastically. 'Are you referring to Latin America? The Mexica? Spanish economics, like the Ottoman were awful. Both made a living from plunder. Huge silver mines, vast troves of gold, hopes of el Dorado. So in went stout Cortes and plundered. Disease was the problem, unintentionally I would argue. The Church, fearing human sacrifice and cannibalism, converted the natives. It is very human to offer belief. Only the ignorant deride salvation. What you should oppose is greed and rapine, not migration or belief. Today's politicians and judiciary fail to understand. They make hatred a crime. How stupid. These people think Christian hatred of sin is not progressive enough. If they want to control the streets, they must first limit immigration to those whose practices are in harmony with theirs, including, or rather excluding paedophilia. Presumably the Civil Service failed because they don't know such behaviours exist.'

'What is the age of consent in Asia?' asked the Scottish boy.

'Colonialism shares good ideas', I replied. 'You've heard about the Arab Spring? It happened in approximately 600 AD.

This led to an exchange of information; a good thing. From India information could travel to Timbuktu. Think globalisation. Advances in maths occurred in a few places like India, Persia, Greece, Babylon, Sumer. Conquer these and transfer all that good practice into a vast and thirsty geography. This worked when religion and language fuelled conquest hand in hand. Sadly the East India Company forbade missionaries and clung narrowly to trade. Holland did much the same in Japan, Brazil and Indonesia. Of course if you believe in Orientalism, a small idea inflated by people with an inferiority complex, you will parse civilisation until nothing is left.'

'Across the world the countries most stressed by loss of bio-diversity and global warming require support, and co-operation, both economic, and political, if COP 28 is to be safeguarded.'

'Does that means co-operating with China?' asked the Scots boy.

I ignored him. 'The only test of any political system is: will it save the planet?' I said. 'The USSR left behind a landscape of strategic failures, a surrealist canvas of abandoned dreams, conceived by well-intentioned communists, who, it turns out, were not strategists, and had no civilisation. Europe stood down their colonies in Africa to get money off the Yanks but offered nothing to take their place save manic dictators lining their pockets, like Mobutu and Kaunda. An alternative would be to install competencies, on the quid pro quo of engagement in COP 28.

'Human greed is the driver of extinction in Nature. In this context hegemony is hardly to the point. The problem is humanity. Not colonies. In fact, colonialism is a rare human activity that brought benefits: Yogi Bear, Coke. You name one.' I said to the children.

And there in the front row was lovely Sacha, smiling at me. 'Go on Sacha, name one.'

'Democracy,' she said.

'A British export designed to make the rich sanctimonious. Our House of Commons makes Etonians prime ministers then sends them to the House of Lords that favours the status quo. If you want democracy copy the Americans. Or change leaders by killing the incumbent judicially, if they lie or cheat. If not, reward them.' I said.

'Rugby,' said Sacha.

'No, no. The death penalty should be constitutional.'

She hunched her shoulders and giggled inexplicably.

'OK' I said. Irish Rugby benefits from colonial style schools set up in Leinster where it is passionately supervised by priests.

'Scandinavians sold Irish women into slavery. Normans did much to advance our countries, as brutal conquerors. They even spread civil society in Scotland giving Normans lands and titles. This was a good counter to uncivilised tribes.'

'Normans also colonised Sicily, joining Christian and Islamic cultures into a unique civilisation. Is that not what we need today?'

'Persia was enriched with Islam. Europe was recolonised by ancient Greece and Rome via the Renaissance, the past colonising the present. What is rarely studied today is the role of the bad hegemon, which strips out the links between religions, ethnicities, and cultures 'til everything disintegrates. A warning sign was the fracture of Yugoslavia. Colonialism needs understanding. It can be the flower of humanity.'

'The British laws against the slave trade transformed the lives of millions. They also abolished death sentences for changing religion. This saved countless apostates. Anyone know what an apostate is?'

'There were twelve apostates,' said a child.

'Well done,' I said and gave her the thumbs up.

'Who has never been colonised? Liberia, Ethiopia, Japan. Liberia is a failed state. Ethiopia is not as great as when Memnon was its king. The Aksum Empire conquered Somalia, Djibouti, Sudan, Yemen, and Saudi Arabia and did some colonising.'

'Chinese democracy is a single ruling party which through research, and consultation meets citizens' needs. The British laid an egg and called it democracy. Even now in too many countries the aim is to feed the pig to gargantuan proportions for a minority to devour. The little people, told to dream, are gathered in for exploitation as required.

'Societies that conquer expand. Their rich get more stuff. This leads to revolution and redistribution rarely to the poor. Conquest breeds refugees, refugees flee and create colonies.

'But all is not lost. The *conquered* stay close to their roots. India is culturally rich and spiritual, as One Star can tell you. Communism is unprincipled, and a form of Darwinism which I detest. The Earth needs protection against humanity, so less greed, less violence, less materialism, less extinction please. Export of ideas, of socialism, of unity, of prosperity please.' I was proud of this lesson, but there would be consequences.

Sure enough Wing Commander Lightly invited me for a drink.

'A G&T? he asked. 'Good to see you. Sorry, there's only me. As you may know I am based in three locations: Brussels, London, and here. The wife's on furlough.'

'Goodness. How grand. I did wonder. You're not really on my screen.'

'I spend a bit of time on the subcontinent. All over actually. Happily, I visited Hong Kong over decades. Had thousands of shirts made there. They never quite mastered buttons particularly their colour.'

My mind wandered. *This man is a peacock* I thought.

'Where did you buy your suits?' I enquired.

'Huntsman. Savile Row.'

'Do they still fit?'

'Alas no. I now lend my skills to commerce and so lunch too well. My waistline has expanded Have you come across this gin? From Marden in Kent?'

'Well, well. I'm not familiar with it.'

'Arabia is bigged up because too much oil is sloshing about. Oil prices give us sleepless nights. The Russians and Arabs putting heads together secretly once again. Like in the seventies. When all is said it's provincial here. You can tell by the range of gins available.'

'Do you know Mrs Goldiwallah?' I interjected.

'Can't say I do.'

'Very lovely woman. I'll ask her to give you a ring. Her husband can get what you want in the way of booze.'

'I'm not bothered. So which bit of archaeology has caught your eye?'

'I am quite taken by pre-Islamic snake worship? And Dilmun, even Bahrein as the Garden of Eden.'

'I've always preferred Armenia. Is everything under control up in Bahrain? Are the Saudis satisfied with the security?'

'No idea.'

'There is one thing. Did you know I have two daughters at the English-Speaking School? One of them came home full of some remarkable recidivist views on the superiority of British colonialism.'

'Ah! You've got me bang to rights. Did you say "came home?"'

'Yes, I'm officially resident here. I was a bit surprised by your observations, and particularly those of your PA.'

'I leave him to it.'

'He claims Israel is a colony of America.'

'Oh dear.'

'He claims American democracy is quite unfit for purpose in developing countries and even in the USA. I wouldn't like you to get into trouble.'

'Very kind. But there is no possibility of that at all. So you don't approve?'

'I don't.'

'How disappointing. Surely colonialism is inevitable?'

'We progressives passionately reject it. We don't buy what France did.'

'North Africa and Vietnam?'

'The French were cruel in Algeria.'

'France is an integrated and majestic nation.'

He looked out of the window. We didn't see eye to eye. *But,* I thought, *we are on the same side. The side of America.* On the other hand Amelia had given him the sack. Despite my misgivings about her, she was not a bad judge of people. I would have to keep an eye on him.

'One Star,' I said later, 'I feel the Research Department would do well to run a rule over the Wing Commander.'

'Yes, sir. Why do they call it the Research Department?'

'Well that's the monicker they used in Oman. It's rather clever don't you think? No-one can deny there is one; few know where it is, what it's really called, what it does, or who runs it.'

Pretty quickly he reported back: 'The Wing Commander is rather less than he claims, and more than he reveals. If things get difficult with the Iranians he is a liability. He seems to have taken the American shilling outside the official system. I'll get him. sir.'

'No, One Star. If he works for America, he's one of the good guys.'

The Ruler demanded I attend his office.

As ever he was frank.

'First and foremost, I want you to sack your personal assistant,' he said.

Knowing his demands tend to evaporate I held my whist.

But he persisted.

'He is fiddling his expenses,' he said. 'This could have repercussions for you personally.

'If he goes, I go'.

'As you know,' he said, 'we are all digesting the inflammatory lesson you gave to the School. I am putting you on notice : cease all Western propaganda. Do not object. Just listen. There are no British founding fathers. Bertram Thomas, Wilfred Mubarak

Thesiger, Saint John Philby are all out of bounds. OK? Burton who wrote racy translations, is also censored.

'Now listen carefully. In the original America, you British died at the hands of your own colonists. Never forget it. In this country we would execute anyone who behaved like that. Violence became the American watchword without proper testing until 9/11. They never washed their hands of it, and still glory in it. Witness the vast output of Hollywood in which stale white cowboys kill Indians In the States rights are still denied to African Americans and Muslims. They are kept out of golf clubs. This is racism. At my prep school I was taught that Roman colonies *conferred* Roman citizenship. This is how to civilise, not the American way of repression, racism and genocide. In short America killed indigenous people, imported poor people and exploited them for profit then set about ruling the world by fighting, looting, and exporting their doubtful version of democracy. At least that's what your PA says. Remember, you work for me; not America.'

'Funnily enough this is what One Star says.'

'I want you to fire him. Israel is seen by Americans as a democratic jewel set amongst undemocratic Arabs, despite the policy of illegal settlements. You Brits tried to keep the region peaceful. But you don't count any more. And you opposed Abdul Nasser, blessed be his name. Britain's reputation as peacemaker, never credible, was extinguished when you joined the USA in the Iraq war.'

'Now here is the text to which you will adhere from henceforth. "America, along with Scandinavians over consume the world's resources. Their large undigested populations of immigrants turn into voting blocs comprising grievance, prejudice, hatred and ignorance, which fester and are poisonous. So American democracy, is at best a feeble way of keeping people quiet.'

None of his arguments made the least impression on me.

'American leaders,' he continued 'are preoccupied by greed. They have achieved one thing which is scale. Ever vaster es-tates, expropriated, or purchased allowed them to strut naked and shameless on the world stage. Revolution threw up greedy leaders. I will only mention the deceased Nixon, Reagan, Kennedy. We will have none of that here. That's the reason I employ you. America was and remains a European project in which Africans and Asians are disadvantaged, but most of all Muslims. So, spy on them, and keep them out.'

'I'm mostly spying on Iran.'

'Why? If I want to know anything I ring them up. So, spy on Oman; they're eccentric. And spy on Pakistan. Don't spy on Saudi as I've just rewritten our agreement.'

'The American version of democracy is superior,' I said crisply.

'Another thing. I have briefed Yahyha to review current tax and employment. When I see American companies here being run out of America they must be taught a lesson. America is past its sell by date. I tell you this in strict confidence. The American food industry is feeding our consumers with excess fat and sugar. Then they send us American consultancies, and American financiers to prise open their competitors in order to achieve outright purchase or over gearing. Logic tells you Arab Pakistani and Indian companies are best equipped to feed our workers. Do they need poor marketing and awful nutrition?'

'Do Americans train our people? No. America long neglected the Middle East and Africa, save for nursing corrupt regimes to extinguish communism. They leant on the colonial powers to abolish colonies, surprise, surprise. So now it is China and Russia who are 'funding' mining companies in Africa, and lending money to build ports and dams America's fixation on hegemony and decolonisation opened China, Africa and the Middle East to vandals. And when China helps itself, they squeal.'

'Across the world others alleviate poverty by socialism with some capitalism. America abolishes socialism. They do not need it as they exploit the world's poor as their external proletariat. They boast equality when inequality feeds ambition. Now they disadvantage Muslims.'

It was at this point the Ruler's handsome features became covered with a film of perspiration, despite the excellent air conditioning.

'Now Mr Research Department,' said he, 'please digest all I have told you and rewrite your job description. You have a week to do so. Oh, and by the way, will you be at Ascot this year?'

I have to say this command reveals that the Ruler is suffering from a rare brain disease.

The news from the West Bank this morning is disturbing. I pray that our American colleagues get this right. Popular opinion in Europe is against further civilian casualties. There is nobody I can talk to about this on a personal level. Except perhaps MacSpity.

His dad came through the area as a sapper between the wars a time of absence: of cold stores, sewage treatment, clean water, hygienic food distribution, air conditioning, so he pushed his son in the direction of cooling it down and cleaning it up. This was long after St John Philby did his deals with the Americans betraying his masters in India. Thesiger was traversing the Empty Quarter without much of a map. According to our Ruler, the Americans unofficially adopted Israel as a colony despite condemning colonies in general. Of course, the background was political manoeuvring, skirmishes and wars. The USA knew their policies would preclude a two State solution until they chose otherwise. One Star wrongly accuses America of denying equality at home as well as in Africa and the Middle East. I believe Americans expect Saudi will lead their Sunni counterparts in the region into cleaning up the mess. But if the solution is to come from bringing Palestinians and Israelis together lubricated by Saudi money the sale of long spoons would have rocketed in the souk.

Back to the young MacSpity. His dad pointed out to him that expats in the Gulf were demanding the higher things in life: sanitation, chilled chicken, and cool air. These are now commodities. Transactions are based on invitations to America's top table.

Air conditioning is still highly valued by Westerners and even some of the locals. Until very recently some used to wrap up in a soaking sheet and lie on the roof beneath the stars, with the promise of bone ache and rheumatism as a consequence.

Punkiwallahs, hi tech in the Middle Ages, were imported from Bombay at a time when impecunious Britons would take a job of political agent as an implausible route to a career. They died like flies from disease and heat, and are now despised by prepubescent students. As in West Africa young men came out destitute and survived briefly wrestling the unknown. Talk about the blind leading the blind. Meanwhile foreign colonials like the Emperor Heliogabalus had snow delivered from the mountains and dug holes to store it in.

The Persian Empire colonised part of the Gulf, introducing the architecture of wind towers, which drew in cool air and gave cities peculiarly graceful silhouettes.

The movies arrived, and Carrier's chiller and central compressor cooled an audience in Times Square for the first time in the 1920s, then by a soft version of colonialism ie financial and diplomatic power, coerced foreigners to buy them. And now the untold millions of Qatar are invested in cooling the great outdoors itself. Dubai has employees with air conditioned jackets, and on a macro scale, reportedly, is trying to air condition a beach and after that the city, if not the world. That would be a nice reversal of colonialism but is unlikely. They will need even more money. The imperial powers had made them rich. I'm not sure if this was the intention. But perhaps this notion of colonialism will make the mindless happier.

The cost is beyond my comprehension. No matter. MacSpity as a young man acquired a reputation for wizardry that only Bill Gates equalled.

MacSpity has the common touch. He raced camels in the old days without the slightest control of his wayward steeds.

The camel doesn't have brakes. Steering in a circle he never wins. He is very British, which apparently is a mistake. Despite the heat he is surprisingly keen on running about. Given his roly-poly physique it is inevitable he gets into fights. I'm not saying Arabs don't fight but they have difficulty understanding how to elide sport and fisticuffs.

Quite a lot of his customers had beards. It was a matter of manners to seize an Arab by his beard and stroke it in a manly but considerate way. This put everyone at ease. I remember introducing him to an old guy who was champion at killing sharks, even in old age. Somehow, they would get a shark into a narrow channel of water. Then the bravest would leap in, straddle the shark and rip open its belly with a knife. Old men convene to get this extravaganza on the road. If for some reason they couldn't find a shark they concealed their disappointment by grabbing each other by the beard. Successful shark riders grabbed beards in the most manly but tender way.

MacSpity has a beautiful wife, Barbara. He asked after my own love life.

'Are you still working on Mrs Goldiwallah?' he asked.

'In progress,' I replied.

'I would think of settling down if I were you. I don't see how a well-connected man does not have a partner, especially in this heat.'

'Is that a recommendation?'

'You know my Barbara. Ours is a true romance. You probably don't know, but I suffer from a minor health problem. Without her |I'd be a goner. What you need is an older version of herself.'

This sounded difficult. 'How do you survive?' I asked.

MacSpity, the most fierce yet endearing of men, looked baffled.

'My advice is fall in love. It is the reason for existence.'

The British consul in Dubai, in days gone by, was addicted to sport, so he designed a golf course at his residence harnessing the artistry of the miniature paintings of Persia, in delicacy, precision and the romance of its conception. His golf course comprised eighteen holes in a site roughly equivalent to a very small garden with a lawn the size of a hanky behind a suburban semi-detached house in Hounslow. But her Majesty's Consul had to accommodate a large generator, a tennis court, a boat, two four-wheel drives and a telegraph pole.

Each fairway intersected with at least two other fairways, often three. Each green was no more than five foot in diameter, and was in fact brown, being comprised of sand and sump oil. Many shots had to surpass the generator, the garage, the tennis court, the boat and a number of other obstacles such as dustbins and even the living quarters in one hit. It was important to restrict the number of people on the course to a dozen and no more at any one time to avoid fatalities.

In Oman my British contacts tend to be military. The victorious campaign in the Jebel Akhdar was conducted by Lofty Large, the Glorious Glocesters, the SAS. Some of their associates subsequently used a golf club known as the Royal Ghala Wentworth near Ruwi.

Prominent in military circles a man called Splash was prepared to live under canvas provided he had access to refreshments and outdated copies of the *Racing Life*. The endless troop of topers at cocktail parties, all faces from Huis Clos, will never become members of my club.

They give no thought to brave boys in khaki sleeping beneath the slow wheel of coruscating stars although the creation of hotels in the Jebel Akhdar puts this in perspective.

The air conditioning fixed, I received news I had been dreading. Amelia my ex was arriving any minute, and I would have to meet her. I say my ex, but that is an exaggeration. In a relationship you feel centre stage, as if everybody knows you are pivotal. When the relationship ceases you may find you are irrelevant. I had made certain by insulting her for what I felt was disloyalty. Long since she had married the Wing Commander and borne him daughters.

I feel distinctly irrelevant.

CHAPTER FIVE

One Star as usual was on top of things.

'Your Amelia is landing tomorrow ETA early. The Research Department is on to it. Her supervisor arrives shortly after; different flight. Begging your pardon – I do not wish to intrude –they have enjoyed a close relationship over the years have they not?'

This is not what I wanted to hear.

'How would I know?' I said.

'I thought…'

'Please have some Roses – Dutch be in her room with a note – welcoming her; my name at the bottom.

'Very well Sir.'

We were destined to meet embarrassingly, painfully. I remember when we broke up, I made a mental note of some verses which applied.

If a star were confin'd into a tomb,
Her captive flames must needs burn there;
But when the hand that lock'd her up, gives room,
She'll shine through all the sphere.

Although I do not like Amelia, these verses stick in my mind.

We met for Coffee in the Burj. Looking at her closely, she did not resemble the carefree joyous spirit I once knew. Yet she was beautiful, iconically. Was it right to superimpose one era onto another? As if people remain the same and memories and prejudices stay identical?

I looked searchingly for the face that had electrified me. The features were recognisable, but the inhabitant had vanished.

She became uncomfortable under my gaze. I took her hand.

'I am so sorry,' I said. 'I do not know how to make things up to you.'

'You have nothing to make up for,' she said stiffly, shaking her head as if she had water in her ear.

'I was upset,' I said, 'as perhaps were you.

'You got my message?'

'That you were very, very angry?'

'I worked hard to get you accepted. None of it matters. We cannot rake over the past, which from the heights we both have climbed is insignificant. I expected trust. You broke up in a forced and ugly way.'

'I thought…'

'We do not need to go over this. I am happily partnering a man who is a high achiever, worth the sum of you and me a hundred times over.'

'Ouch. He must be an inspiration. You have children which I wanted. And they are beautiful.'

'Really? They are not the be all and end all of life. I surrendered them in the divorce which was *au fond amicable*.'

'You and I perhaps did not talk enough.'

'What? Us? I never bilked at anything.'

'I don't want to upset you. And yet… And yet I felt we had a sort of contract. That you would help. Instead you hindered.'

'No,' she replied. 'Things aren't like that in the real world. In a relationship each gives ground. Anyway you look good and I'm sure you've found happiness. Tell me what's happening in Gaza.'

'It is what it is. Both sides are trapped in the logic of that situation. The Americans will sort it.'

'You think. It is a tragedy.'

'The experience on both sides must be unbearable.'

'And what does art say? What does religion say…?'

'I don't know. I would ask old friends like Hazlitt. He is good on art.'

'You're still dabbling…?'

'Oh yes. Don't know what I would do without it.'

'As I thought, you do not understand.'

'I feel impotent. It is outside my hands.'

She sighed, gazed upwards. 'Do you have to?'

'When we broke up I started to see a black disk, in my mind. Eyes open, eyes closed. I was going mad.'

'Poor you.'

'I was in love, utterly. But when I look back…'

'Yes?'

'It was the real thing. The nearest I have come to reality. I found the culprit. It was me. The distrust, the disbelief, the cowardice were mine. They formed a weather system. You became invisible, my imperfections clear. But at the heel of the hunt I loved you utterly.'

The strange thing is my urgent pleas began to ignite an urge within me.

I took her hand. 'I don't know why you say these things. It is all too late,' she said, and something obdurate in her face displaced her usual serenity.

'I owe your mother,' I said. 'All those years ago.'

'You do not know, she passed away?'

'She loved you so very much.'

'She was ashamed of me. She thought me fast and loose. She wished with all her heart you and I had stayed together.'

And then despite my outpouring of contrition I found this notion, that her mother had once favoured me, utterly unbelievable. As if everything in life was untrue, my character, my ambitions, Amelia herself, all part of a story so slight, so meaningless the details could be changed without repercussion.

'You look aghast,' she said.

Aghast? What a choice of word, I thought. *Useful in romantic stories.*

'Mummy bought me a flat in the Kings Road. So I might forget.'

She was right was she not? A mother's love is everything.

'Oh. You mean love as in d'Arcy's enormous house. You had no money. I don't work like that. In retrospect you were a passing fancy. Not to be sniffed at, but part of the ephemera I collect. You know full well I don't believe in anything.'

'You do. Science explains you. The things that obsess me, religion, love, death, seem to fall through the cracks, don't they?'

At that moment I was really thinking her dismissal of religion and art is quite possibly psychopathic. Cold blind science is nothing without insight.

'What nonsense,' she said. 'Death is ubiquitous and explains Life. Your kind of love and your kind of religion do not.'

'Disease then.'

'Yes, disease is a marker and an explanation, which is why I study it. Pavlov got me thinking. I see religion, and politics, as processes. In the case of religion a process of mass conversion, and mind control by the Jesuits. The sheer scale allows analysis. In Africa population density and migrations destabilise societies, unleashing sorcery and witchcraft. I turned to politics and studied China. They led in mind control and political conversion. Seriously I would have a check-up if I were you. You show some hall marks of brain disease.'

'I don't think so.'

'Have you read Sargeant's Battle for the Mind?'

'Religion and love engross me. Not your thing.'

'The degradation of the Natural world increases famine, disease, and. an ever increasing quantum of data. Behaviour must be controlled. Starting with benchmarks from the Mao era we study mass conversion. The terror of extinction when COP 28 fails –as it will- may bring the majority to their senses but will require coercion.'

She continued drily as if giving a lecture: 'More recently work on the biome reveals microbes in their millions determining dietary preferences as well as illnesses. Immunology shows different resistance across species. This will predict the fate of peoples and life on the planet. Your sexual preferences and identities are irrelevant.'

'And do you know how those processes work in the brain?'

'Not completely, but I hope to contribute. Funnily enough my interest was triggered by my then husband. I was fascinated, I can tell you. One of the reasons we broke up was he insisted on me being his nurse. He suffered a contretemps with a Tiger Moth years ago, got a bang on the head. At a lowly level I am semi expert on the subject. You may not know this but fits are not infrequently associated with minute fragments of bone in the brain.'

'Caused by Tiger Moths?'

A faraway look came into her eyes.

Not wanting to be outdone I said: 'I am even more religious now.' I gave her my most mysterious gaze and heard the pompous drawl in my voice.

'It is in places like this,' she said, 'that these religions were invented. We were trapped by the Middle East. I prefer India and Ambaji.'

'In that we are still one,' I said breathlessly.

She winced. And took her hand from mine.

'Your priests,' she said, 'and your gurus were mired in folklore, primitivism, and boys' games. Their outdated rules discredit them. Even Africa is heavily into ancestor worship which privileges men.'

'And,' she added, 'I despise the school which invented orientalism.'

I tried to mollify her, and conceded Iran was nothing to write home about, but, I suggested the prophets who acquired and refined their medicine, and astronomy from older civilisations, can be proud of the acculturation of their world.

'I think them primitive, in their treatment of women,' she replied sharply. 'Persia was raped by America. Britain joined the gang bang, hoping as per usual for a pay-off, despite its impotence of latter days.'

'You are too harsh. Anyway, my job entails keeping an eye on them.'

'I don't like the sound of that,' she said.

In the real world created by history the Western powers seek domination. I peep for them. Can we meet again soon?'

'Absolutely not,' she said coldly.

'Did you ever read James Elroy Flecker?' I asked, gently taking her hand in mine.

'You know I can't compete with you on the literary front.'

'He wrote doggerel verse. "Men are unwise. And curiously planned. They take the Golden Road to Samarkand."'

'That's it? What on earth does it mean?'

'In a far country it was always hot and difficult to grow food. Wide deserts and high mountains meant there was little to live on. The river dried up, as did trade. The sea lapping upon another shore in another country, shrank.'

'A great Emperor came and conquered. He made a vast system of irrigation which enabled the people to grow crops. The irrigation was fed by the shrinking sea. Salt leached into the earth. Desolation followed. Yet the men were happy when the land degraded. They once had nothing. Now with nothing they remember life's purpose.'

'That's it?'

'That's it.'

'I suppose this country was Samarkand.'

'My Samarkand is an imaginary place.'

'You live in isolation. It seems to be punishing you.'

'I find the people interesting. The Iranians on the other hand are excellent enemies.'

'Is that what you do for a living? Make enemies?'

'These people are not democratic.'

'I don't remember you as prejudiced.'

'Think of the great cultures. All took their gifts from racial springs. Semites, Germans, Russians. Some built walls against interbreeding.'

'In Britain you can be jailed for such nonsense.'

'Prejudice merely means judging things early, as early as you can before you lose. Judging is a failing science since it was forbidden. Nature is in distress,' I said. 'Your scientific duty is to rescue her. I spend hours looking for beauty in silicates, capturing her last moments. I see it as man's legacy. That is the role of art.'

I congratulated myself. I had kept my head.

Her Professor flew in. The Research Department prepared some notes for me. He appeared to be a past master at conspiracy and double dealing. He slept intermittently with Amelia and others.

His name was Hughes Hallett. He was a confidant of leading figures in Republican America. A man with strong political connections in Israel and apparently with the Russians, who was now trying to open a line of enquiry with the Iranians. A lover of Africa and all things African, so he pretended. I doubted it. Amelia benefitted from his interests: immunology, the Biome, viruses.

I did not seek an opportunity to meet him.

She had been at the Hygiene and Tropical when we were an item. I took a coffee with her as the Professor was ferried from the airport.

'You were a step ahead of me intellectually.'

'Such nonsense; nobody who really knows me would say I have any intellect. You always undersold yourself and under-performed at work. I do what pleases me. Like a man.'

'I betrayed you. There is no other way of putting it. And then I took the road to Samarkand, unwise but brave.'

'What is that supposed to mean again?'

'Samarkand is a male destination. Risks do not compute and do not correlate to outcome. Departure has no significance. Destination has no meaning. What we invest in is holy and means everything. It is a trope for an idea that men above all are drawn to, which calls for audacity, resolution in the face of death, an Odyssean alertness. To be polytropos, wily, to have an open heart, and an unwavering love of Nature, which faces extinction.'

She looked at me from half closed eyes. 'Back in the motherland,' she said, 'which you have absented far too long, that kind of sexism doesn't wash. You have gone native or mad. Probably both. The opposite of your Samarkand is my world of reason.'

'Charan Singh, my hero,' I replied, 'came from peasant stock and knew malnutrition, terminal indebtedness and the dreadful evictions of peasants. Is that materialist enough for you?'

'There is not enough arable land, not just in India.'

'The Chinese took theirs by the scruff of the neck. The Indians tried politics. Singh legislated for more equitable land holding and tried to avoid violence. He was a Gandhi man, a Tolstoy man. Far sighted, painstaking. He knew the peasant to be magnificent; carrying the iron weight of toil; and the total indifference of their rulers. Malaria, and starvation are their lot. From Africa to Italy to Russia.'

'But look what the Russians did,' she cried. 'Instead of narrowing the gap they killed Kulaks and collectivised and evicted peasants. Bugger off to Samarkand and leave the problem for science to solve.'

That was unpleasant.

'I've brought something for you,' I said hurriedly. I had a large picture wrapped up in brown paper: a picture I had painted of the Queen of Sheba meeting Solomon as her equal.

'This is my gift to you. My ruler finds it vulgar,' I said. 'But it shows off the desert to effect, don't you think? What do you make of her? To the Arabs she was Bilqis. To the Ethiopians, Makeda.'

'Outside my zone.'

'She ruled Sabaa in south western Arabia; she worshipped the sun and her caravan carried gold, jewels, and spices.

Frankincense was grown in her country. She wanted to ask Solomon riddles. He learned this from one of his birds, a hoopoe, a creature capable of divination and an expert in revealing secret springs and wells. Hoopoes were used in Bahrain which is stiff with fresh water springs, on land, and in the sea. The Hoopoe is magical; it has medicinal properties in its body and is associated with kingship and with Solomon, who was a high priest and brought secret knowledge to mankind. There are ten million Hoopoes, but our Research Department confirms they will soon be extinct like so many other birds. How do you like my Bilqis? In the painting I mean?'

'It means nothing to me.'

She had completely lost interest.

'See. She is showing a leg from beneath her dress. The Arabs say she had hairy legs. And the hooves of an ass. Solomon's Djinn told him this. Solomon had a glass floor made before his throne and she, thinking it was water, lifted her skirts and revealed her legs. Solomon ordered his Djinn to create a depilatory for her. He then made a pass at her. Successfully, so they say.'

'These are worthless fairy tales.'

'The Ethiopians say he tricked her into his bed and made her pregnant and in Saba'a she bore Solomon Menilekan who became king of Ethiopia. He was really the Memnon known as Ethiope's king, the greatest of Troy's champions, and the first black prince to triumph.'

Disappointed by her reaction I went on:

'The Ethiopians were one of the first countries to practice agriculture including cereals and grains. And while much of the middle east was starting to desertify the Ethiopians, the Cushitic and Omotic peoples as well as Semites cultivated their land wonderfully well. Apart from Aksum they established the kingdom of D'mt to the west, a land of ivory, tortoise shell, rhinoceros horn, gold, silver, slaves.'

I had failed to read the warning signs. I am, it seems, a one trick pony.

Perhaps I thought the exotic tale of Bilqis might have unsettled her and made her respect my world of the imagination, of metaphors which have the power to unlock the psyche. I failed. I tried to make up lost ground.

'I am impressed by your work on brain disease.'

'I found an association with tiny abnormalities,' she replied, 'the origins of which may be trauma, or a number of diseases. It is not always capable of diagnosis. Of course, people like you bang on about an interface between the material and non-material worlds.'

This aroused in me a tenderness towards her. I imagined Amelia trapped in her material world, unable to escape, unable to find love.

'When you talk of these romantic notions of Samarkand, where geography induces psychosis, do you entertain the idea that aberrant electrical discharges correlate with your religion?'

'I do,' I replied.

'I mean reduce it to neurobiology. Even you must find patriarchal religion irritating. Epileptic prophets in clouds of fire and earthquakes in the Old Testament? A female warrior envisioning saints and angels, triggered by bells. In most cases, like my ex-husband, falling over.'

'Poor Lightly. And how did you access the data?'

'Research projects, papers.'

But you discount religion?'

'There is good evidence to show delusions associated with preictal prodromes, or the ictal event or post ictal psychosis or an interictal personality trait. Are you familiar with the geschwind syndrome?'

'Not at all.'

'Dostoevsky saying that Heaven was going down upon the earth. It engulfed me, he said. I have really touched God. You healthy people can't imagine the happiness I feel before a fit, he said.'

'Your husband said that? I've met him you know.'

'Dostoevsky said it, inhaling a narcissus flower as a cure.'

'Ah. Progressive medicine?'

'I was not referring to medicine. The Christian tradition is misleading. Falling on the ground and rolling about are recorded in the context of demons. The word in Greek is possession, seizure.'

'There are fears that the Chinese Communist party will use AI to analyse facial expressions and brain signals to check loyalty. Science must think carefully about AI for the sake of the laity.'

'Americans exaggerate,' I said. And then felt guilty.

Later when I reflected on my conversation with Amelia I was depressed. Yet I could only admire the breadth of her work. And against my better judgement I found myself imagining her feelings when I had dumped her. She probably has a scientific explanation: of love of religion, in some pending file. Are either in any sense a disease?

I was lying in bed with Mrs Goldiwallah. I like her a lot, though she stank of oriental perfume.

'Do you love your husband?' I asked her.

She grinned mischievously. 'What is love?' she asked. 'Obviously I don't have to love him. But I do love him, yes. More than you do,' she said and laughed hugely. Then she said with unnecessary intimacy: 'Dylan?'

'I suppose you want me to call you by your first name now,' I sighed, 'which I have shamefully forgotten.'

She looked brave yet dejected.

'I am Morgiana. Don't tease.'

'Ah Morgiana. Reminds me of a sports car I once had. And yet you are sumptuously young. Why are you here?' I asked.

'To please you and me both. Oh, I see. Well, he is mad to make money.'

'How?'

'If you are nice, I will tell you. As for me, I am here because it pleases me better than there.'

'This is a tectonic plate we're riding,' I said. 'Can you feel it move?'

'Only when, you know…' And she guffawed again.

'No, but do you not feel there is an invisible space that shimmers somewhere between east and west; sometimes on the sea, sometimes on land? It divides two realities, doesn't it? Just now the tectonic plate is ours. But they have theirs, those people on the other side. They are different. They are more moral than people here in their dedication and sense of purpose. I oppose them of course. But we Westerners disqualify ourselves from judging. Poor saps, aren't we?'

'Who are the Iranians?' She replied. 'I am divided. There is no doubt that their ways are satisfying to them. But when things broke apart? The Persians were always different from everybody else. Don't you think?'

'Everyone's the same.'

'What the Arabs created was enormous wasn't it?'

'How?'

'I can't exactly say. To use a sporting metaphor, it was momentum. They invaded. They fought like tigers. But they were pragmatic. Then came the Turkic lot. Once they had scope and scale, they were able to leverage a vast amount of assets. From mathematics to architecture; from philosophy to war. By conquest and wonderful language they standardised the loot of history, until, almost without thinking, they moved ideas and facts around. Of course, the One God helps.'

'You could be talking of the Jews.'

'Hardly. They were founding fathers perhaps. But if I am right the best civilisation was Persian, in culture, art, and poetry, and the legacy of mathematics, astronomy, medicine. But both Israel and Iran feel themselves to be victims, oppressed but right. They have much in common. I know all about this. Looking for victims is a core skill in espionage. The thing that confuses me is the Iranian heritage of worship is a source of power, the opposite of victimhood, which confronts the West. Long ago the Iranians saw through Americans, and like them live more fully by reviling their enemies.'

'America is the referee,' she said.

I patted her on the head, and continued:

'Scholars turned out to be Persian. Grammar, law, science, literature, philosophy, art. Persian. It was almost a reverse takeover.'

'They were wonderful, I suppose. The West is still in denial?'

'Probably,' I said.

Then to my discomfort, she snuggled up to me.

'In the West we achieved wondrous things ourselves, in art music and technology. Without your help.'

'And feminism,' she added.

'A dubious path, unless you're talking of the four backed beast. This peninsula is patriarchal,' I continued. 'Let's leave it at that. But we learned from Persia and Arabia Love, and Chivalry.'

'Sufi poetry?' she said. There is more to her than meets the eye.

'The Duke of Aquitaine, Compte de Poitiers, created the poetry of love, a sort of Troubador. Where did he get it? He had been in Palestine. Afterwards love poetry flowered in Andaluse. The exaltation of the beloved, the exaltation of you Mrs Goldiwallah, my beloved, my much beloved. The Muwashshah school which had its roots in Arab poetry fed into this European awakening. That's how much we owe you. Like astronomy and mathematics, love and gallantry took seed in rough arsed Europe. The flowers of Donne grew out of his versatile rough arse. Where Christianity and Judaism had room to breathe, synergy between West and East increased. Some ended up loving more stylishly and more soulfully. Have you read 1001 Nights?'

'No. At least what I read was very, very rude, also racist, and sexist.'

'It is rude, but I put that down to the translator Burton. He was fleshly. But it was Arab and Indian in its origins was it not? Mainly? The Persians on the other hand were more refined. Their lovely cartoons and their poets; Rumi is so popular in the USA I am told. So why is it we do not celebrate these diversities and rapprochements?'

'Condescension?'

'Persians, having an inferiority complex, spend too much time being awkward.'

'Time for me to get up,' said Mrs Goldiwallah. She seemed a little more broad beamed when she was up than when she was down.

I was fortunate. All those men locked down together in Masirah, an island from which it was not possible to escape, where there was nothing much to do except drink, (I hope) reminded me how lucky I was. Then there were the oil installations and the military. Men cooped up in droves, alienated from normal society, let alone the indigenous people thinly etiolated down this inhospitable coast.

CHAPTER SIX

Despite the Ruler's admonitions I did my best to justify my relationship with MacSpity. He had done enormous installations for the military and oil industry. Round, very white, with an aquiline profile and a rolling gait, he was a masculine sort of cove. Not tall, he had a kind of physicality that suggested he was no slouch with his fists.

Back in the office the Research Department had thrown up fresh info on Amelia, her research into biota, and its impact on appetite, health, and even life itself, intersecting with her work on the immune system. She was in a close relationship with her supervisor. I am not remotely jealous. The Research Department spelled out her life in unnecessary detail but left out her expertise in brain disease. Hardly gets a mention. Meanwhile I was working on the Ruler's pet project, controlling terrorism in Eastern Arabia, but funded locally. The project leader, at an operational level, bin Khalifa, is xenophobic, clever and has a massive network of contacts including Canada and Ghana.

Iran (the IRGC) wished to buy Amelia's secrets. So did Saudi. Was this about biological warfare? There appeared to be simple triggers which suppress or heighten the immune system. But I couldn't get my hands on what exactly. Certain biota charged up immunity or changed it with lethal consequences.

The Iranians, the briefing document said, were exceptionally clever players who, blunted by theocracy, were disgruntled. But, as always, they would do anything to get one over the Americans.

This had almost certainly been written by a team containing who knows how many people of second or third generation Iranian blood. I settled down to paperwork, occasionally going into Oman to clock the monsoon. I calculated the pros and cons of negotiating the purchase of Amelia's secrets. And in the way one does when stressed I listened to dreams. I dream that I am a father, albeit rather old.

I heard that some high powered visitation from a terror group was happening in Oman, surprising since they were not welcome there, and it was well policed. I made a trip, checking venues and contacting people. The Omanis stood somewhat above the fury of Gaza.

In Muttrah you could glimpse people piss and shit, behind the rocks.

In Muscat, look at the names of ships which anchored there, the sailors climbed up cliffs to paint the rock face, with vessels' names, right up to the foreland. I looked at the old palace so much nicer than Alice's.

On the way back, driving my old Mercedes, I stopped outside Ruwi for the night. I stood beside the hotel swimming pool. I looked across. Only a few yards away lay the children's paddling pool, no more than eighteen inches deep. Then I noticed a child lying on its back. Was he playing? Could he be just underneath the surface? I ran up. I lifted him out. Like a little doll. 'Oh My Christ,' I yelled. Inexplicably the little one was dead; drowned.

My dreams of fatherhood would cease.

I had to stay another day to help the police.

Before I went home I visit the house of an old man, a Twelver, who never drank tea. If you drank in the day, he said, you perspire at night. Once it started, it would never end.

'What does that do to your kidneys?'

He smiled the most gentle smile.

'How are you,' I asked. 'Salaam aleikum, kaif sahtak?'

'Al hamdullillah.'

'Do you still have no air conditioning?' I asked. He used to sleep on the flat roof of his house in soaking sheets after wrapping his body in them before sleep. He didn't invite me into his house as it would be inappropriate for me to see his wife. She, poor thing, dressed all in black was a subterranean creature, a troglodyte in his dark close cavern, her companions invariably other women clad in black. I gave him a little present. He had given me many.

And then One Star announced that both Amelia and Roy had returned. There was a voice mail for me.

'Would you care to meet us for a drink at our apartment?'

She poured me a beer. And looked lovely. My heart ached. He fussed about, as if hospitable. He did the talking but I failed to understand.

At one point he said: 'We need better contacts in Iran. We would like to involve you. You know the people. Could you arrange it for us?'

'I will ask around. I don't want to be involved unless a sale is on. You know better than I that things are hotting up round here. My American friends are convinced the Ayatollah is scheming. I don't see it like that. But you would do well to steer clear.'

Maybe I will consult old Esa, I thought, blocking out the man's dry condescending voice. Failing to pay attention, I nearly fell asleep.

Hughes Hallett now thought I was deaf. He raised his voice. 'Amelia told me your trope of going to Samarkand. I found it intriguing. Let me get this right. It is a male thing. To do with the unknown? High risk? Where bravery must count? Are you up for that? Really?'

'I know what protects the tribe.'

'And your tribe is?'

I bit my tongue.

'It is not very well thought out,' I say in a conciliatory way. 'Maybe it involves deceit, which I'm not good at. But I can negotiate a complex deal. I'm not a betting man, but I understand how to calculate the odds. I wouldn't be much use unless you need to sell your property? Why don't you spell out what you have for sale?'

'I thought you better than that. Religion seems so unproductive,' said Amelia.

'In deference to you I classify Love and Religion as diseases, perhaps mirrors reflecting one another. Reflections invisible to you scientists. Symbiosis is the way to go if we wish to rescue this planet. This one.

I will discuss brain disease with you another day, if you co-operate.'

I turn to her Supervisor. 'You know we were once good friends?'

'I do.'

'When talking in that Oriental way, is it on behalf of your employer?'

'Always.'

'Do you think Love is a disease? Is Religion associated with violence?'

'Christianity survived capture by the Roman Empire. Rome attracted barbarous tribes and pacified them. The Carolingians pretended to remake the Roman Empire as the centre of true Christianity. They failed. Just as now America pretends and fails.' I don't know where my casual superficial remarks come from.

One of the girls disappears. Amelia doesn't visit them, so is blissfully unaware.

The Wing Commander is away on a trip. I only hear about the child's disappearance because One Star picked it up from the daily brief.

'That is one of the children you tell fairy stories to,' he says.

'Such beautiful children,' I reply. His face is suffused although whether this is embarrassment or disapproval I do not know.

I go round to their apartment. A policeman is at the door. He snaps to attention. I signal to him to relax.

The child's stepmother invites me in. 'My husband is away,' she says. She sounds heartbroken and humiliated. 'There is a demand,' she says.

'Money?'

She nods and gulps.

'It doesn't sound professional,' I say. 'Shall I liaise with the authorities for you?'

'I am at a loss,' she says. She looks very young not least for the Wing Commander. I touch her arm to provide reassurance. 'I'll be back soon,' I say. 'Do not worry.'

I check with the Department. The child is somewhere in Abu Dhabi, we think. Probably nearby. The amount they want is chicken feed. A conspiracy is confirmed. The kidnapping is a solo run and separate. The search moves south.

Al Qaeda have a high level of involvement in Yemen. I volunteer to do the search. *Is it a coincidence that I am required to go there at this particular time and on my own?* I ask myself. One Star has warned me not to go to Oman. A price on my head, he suggests. He could not have known that all this would happen.

Seen through the child's eyes it must all seem inexplicable. Night time under the full moon, which is utterly beautiful. The breathtaking stars and the breathtaking fear of an abduction.

She witnesses a meeting between people devoted and religious, treating one of their number as a prophet. He blesses his followers.

Someone is brought struggling into the firelight at Ras-Al Had. It is me. I am recognised. But my involvement is of no interest to them. My *amour propre* is hurt. The child is set free but not by me. The ransom is brushed aside.

We return in the night. One Star is driving. The child falls asleep almost on top of me. She seems cheerful; I could fall in love with her.

I am nursing humiliation and depression. Caught between two stools. If Amelia would only meet me halfway we could reach a modicum of mutual respect.

There is no sign of any such move on her part. Why is she and her ridiculous Professor harassing me? Unless they are hiding their intentions. I no longer love her. How can I do my job yet get embroiled?

She doesn't even know my security status. Does she?

The child stirs and wakes up crying. I pet her.

'There, there,' I say softly. 'What is the matter?'

'I want my mummy.'

Which one? I wonder.

Shall I tell you a story?' says One Star at the wheel.

'All right,' she says. 'Thank you.'

'Won't interfere with your driving, will it?'

He ignores me.

'There was a Vizier?' he asks.

She nods.

'A Vizier fell in love with a rich woman. He wooed her and bought her a palace bigger that the Sultan's.'

'Not that story.'

'Go on. Let him,' I say.

'All right then.'

'The rich woman, no more enamoured of her husband, persuades the Caliph to arrest him. She wants the pleasures that she needs. The Vizier employs a Djinn to make his wife great with child.'

'What does that mean?'

'He made her have a baby?' I interjected. 'Half Djinn, half human? Isn't that right One Star?

'Yeah.'

'The child grows up to be a Princess,' he continued. 'She is beautiful but spoiled. She loves living with her mother. Sometimes if she feels lonely, she lies on her couch of whitest ivory, inlaid with pearls and jacinths, and when she sits before her mirror she watches herself chemised with hair shining as if she were the full moon, rising over the Eastern horizon, with flower-white brow and suggestion on her cheeks of anemones.'

'That's lovely.'

'It must have been in Sana'a,' I said. 'So much better then than now.'

'Much better,' said One Star.

'She realises one day she will be lonely. So she decides to find a Prince, to make herself happy. She found an ordinary man who was full of hope. She promises him not only money but happiness, if he does as men must do. Always.'

'What is stipulate?'

'Make a rule. She agreed to protect him,' One Star explained.

'For a year and a day, the young man was sent into another country. On a brief visit, he asks the daughter to marry him. She says no. "My mother," she says, "has made other arrangements." "You must see me," he says. "Out of the question," she says. "You made a promise." "No," she replies, "I am not dependent on you." And she laughs.

"If you deny me," he said |'you will suffer your whole life. It takes a true woman to know selfless love, a gift beyond anything in the world. It is a sin to lose it."

'But she ignored him, and to make things worse she told all her friends. Her mother now promised many things. "I will give you your own palace and all the jewels you want. With such riches you can have anyone in the world." So the daughter refused to see the Prince ever again.'

'But the Prince came with an army. He took the mother prisoner.'

I looked anxiously at Sacha.

'He chopped off her head.'

She smiled.

'Then he locked the daughter in a tower. Her only hope of escape was if a knight errant fell in love with her.'

'What is errant?'

'Making mistakes. Then a knight errant in search of an adventure came along. She let her hair down and he used it to climb the tall tower, and fell in love, and rescued her.'

'That was excellent', said our audience. 'Much better than last time.'

'Yes, I think so too,' I said and stroked her hair. 'Would you like the story of the Caliph once again?'

'Yes,' she said. She was sitting bolt upright now, and her eyes were shining in the moonlight, which scattered through the car. It was as if magic were afoot.

Now I became the storyteller. Caliph Harun al –Rashid bought his wife apples, then noticed a slave had one of them. The Caliph cut his wife into tiny pieces except the head, which he put into a jar. That was best practice. This is what we call an archetype which informs culture and imagery. He guesses he has done wrong. He breaks down. He weeps.

Long, long have I bewailed the sev'rance of our love he cries.

With tears that from my lids stream down like burning rain.

I vow love will unite us. Lips will never speak of severance again:

Joy o'erwhelms yet that which gladdens me makes me to weeping fain.

Tears are now habit, O my eyes, So weep for gladness as for pain.

'Is that a good poem or what?' I asked. 'I got it from Burton.'

'Oh yes,' she said ecstatically. 'It is a good poem.'

'You are going to have a queue of princes waiting to marry you,' I said.

But I thought with satisfaction she is learning about love.

What happened next was illogical. An attempt was made to kill me. A bomb went off under my car. But I was in bed asleep. Maybe it was a warning.

As a consequence I am having nightmares. Three great birds circling overhead hang over me. I am terrified. They were creatures without pity. And when I woke I found myself worrying about Yemen. The people are tough and gave the British a seeing to. Apart from weapons and a shared distaste for Saudi which commend the Iranians to them what did they want? I suspect America has enraged them.

The Ruler summoned me.

'I want data on the Wing Commander. He reports to the Israelis?'

'No way,' I replied.

'Should we lose you, it would be a pity. But there we are.'

'Thank you,' I said.

I feel no more anxiety. I have begun to hope again. After so long a famine? With one I had abandoned.

I will take the girls to meet their real mother and engineer their reconciliation. At the worst they will be grateful. It will be Christian.

I will work on a painting after Cezanne, of a desert palm tree in a valley of shining cubes and rhomboids painted in a palette of ivory, yellow ochre, and mauve, colours subtly depicting what only I can see.

The very act of painting is male, I think. It reveals to me a version of the Arab world in which man is at the centre, lord of women, of children, and the land around them, fortifications, mud daubed prisons, built in the deep past. Philby's father betrayed Britain. His world was autarchy, tribalism, selfishness, conquest, oil. He betrayed us to America. For once I began to question my job.

CHAPTER SEVEN

One Star rang me at 11.00 that night.

'I've had him on the blower again,' he said. Your sparring partner from Iran. He wants to have a chat. I told him your diary is chocka, except twenty minutes midmorning. Got to ring back first thing. Is that OK?'

'No, that's fine. Does he want something?'

'A Westerner to be picked up in Teheran. Wants you to give the OK.'

At 11.00 Esa blew in.

'Number one!' he says cordially.

'Esa. Such a pleasure.'

'Just wanted to clear with you. We expect to arrest an engineer called Edwards this afternoon. Works for an American outfit called Westfall based in Dubai. Iranian wife. Always in and out of the country. The Guards had their eye on them for ages. Do you have any concerns?'

'As if I can control anything like that.'

'I look to you for advice.'

'I don't know about American intentions. What can we do?'

'If the wife shows she will be picked up too.'

'Of course. Anything you want me to do?'

'I heard you held a meeting with the Wing Commander.'

'I have nothing on him.'

'Is he a spy? I hear there's something wrong with him. He is possessed.'

'He has assets down in Masirah. Presumably to fly over your way. Is your Russian kit up to it?'

'We are like you in the blitz. Ready to take on any hardship. Never surrender. Our friends the Russians are doing what makes sense.'

'My PA insists Russia was created by the West. Napoleon taught them revolution and the slime between intellect and perfidy. He says the Germans taught them genocide.'

'The Wing Commander worries us. He reports to America. They don't control anybody now least of all your new best friend, the Crown Prince.'

'I'll get back to you.'

'You are in danger. Watch out!' Esa smiled. 'Israel is everywhere. Another thing. This high-powered researcher?'

'Ah. Amelia?'

'We like what's she doing. We would have some of it. The immune system could be a real asset. So let her have her head.'

I laugh in a good-natured way.

He shrugs. We wish to talk to her.

'On that one you will need my compliance. I have my eye on you.'

'You know how restrained we are,' he said. 'Every time Israel want more from America they pick off our people. We know the script. Look, they say to the Americans, you must crush Iran. Or Iran will steal the Middle East. We are, how you say, their 'straw man'. America is led by the nose. *You* know how careful we are. last week; Israelis took out one of ours in Beirut last week. It is your duty to inform your ruler that we are on a tight rein. America thinks they control us. Hizbollah is Iran. America will start the next big war if they touch Hizbollah.'

'OK,' I said.

Deciding to tell Amelia about the abduction, I expected a bollocking.

I rang her.

'May I come round? I have some details on Sacha's adventure. Don't be alarmed. Things are under control.'

'Have you spoken to her father?'

'Only the stepmother. But I didn't want you left out.'

'Well, come round if you must. You will find Roy here.'

As soon as I arrived I sat myself down opposite her and told her what had taken place. Naturally my report placed me centre stage. My involvement, I explained, is chance. In the right place at the right time. I was asked to help. Her stepmother was waiting outside the school gate. How they missed each other I don't understand. She was upset.

I spoke to the Wing Commander. I told him we picked her up last night. She had been taken to the interior. She is safe and well. I personally picked her up. At the outset I asked the Wing Commander to provide surety. 75000 US dollars.

'Is that all?'

'We were funding a bigger deal. The Wingco contribution made it easier to separate the legal entities involved. For reasons beyond my pay grade a high-ranking malcontent was identified. Usual stuff. Kidnap, inciting illegal activities in another jurisdiction. It was just bad luck that a freebooter linked two different felonies.

'Just between us it seems a political deal has been struck which permits this terrorist organisation to redeploy assets in the region. What's in it for the countries concerned I don't know. Will these people ever learn?

'Anyway there are sensitivities about bankrolling. For reasons, again outside my ken, a demand for $7,000,000 was made for, as it turns out, nothing at all. Just a diplomatic message I suppose.'

'I can't think why but I feel your ex-husband may know more than I do. Does that sound plausible? I am puzzled why some entrepreneur snatched your daughter. Seems like UDI.

I set off south to Ras Al-Had, with my man, One Star who happens to be good with children.

The pickup was to take place in the early hours on the beach. We parked next to the al Hajar lagoon some way off. We walked over followed by a vehicle. Set up a little bivouac. We were unarmed.

The rest as they say is history.'

'Well thank you for that,' she said without betraying a scintilla of emotion. 'I feel outrage that the authorities in this godforsaken place should have allowed such a thing to happen.'

I thanked her and promised a report once all the facts were known.

'By the way has your ex any health problems?'

'Why?'

'I heard he was off games. A reliable report. Actually I was told he has the holy disease. Does that mean anything?'

'First I've heard. He was fine back then.'

Back in the office I ran through last night's events.

When we got there, we walked secretively down by the sea. I was at once on tenterhooks yet super aware of the canopy overhead. The stars, their extraordinary clarity, in the seemingly infinite breadth of the heavens, were glowing with preternatural moonlight and starlight. No wonder the Arab world was preoccupied with night and the treasure of God's creation. I poor soul am enveloped by my cloudy past.

Everything was silent except random clues of life but none human. The occasional bark of a fox and the unexpected shrill of some bird. Creatures were awake everywhere, I realised. They were waiting hungrily for tiny creatures hatching in the sand and clumsily struggling towards the sea. It was the hatching hour of turtle, that by their routines, inherited from two hundred million years take on crabs, seagulls, crows, foxes, sharks all slavering to eat them. Those that escape would slowly swim the oceans until their alarm would ring and redirect them to this indigo harbour to lay their own eggs in turn. Why? This was not some mechanistic ritual but the celebration of life and as the locals would have it, blessed by God glorious be his name. Below us the waves seemed to sparkle phosphorescent blue. My thoughts turned to Vaughan who saw in a glass darkly, and rove in the mighty and eternal light, both winged and free.

But now the sound of footsteps that worried me, faint splashings, the sound of boot on stones. *How is little Sacha* I wondered? If she is harmed I will wreak havoc. I had a knife.

She must be nearby. Like the turtle everything is against her. For a moment she became one with her mother. Love spilt and touched me. Our second car was parked at Ras al-Jinz.

Little did I know but she was sat in a huge Dodge off roadster in Ras al-Had. There was no gag put on her mouth. No ropes on her limbs. Just a man from Kerala to keep an eye on her. There was a small fire crackling fifty metres away and a group of men staring into the darkness.

Every now and then they would smile and shake each other's hands. 'It's going great,' said the Keralite. 'You want a drink?'

She shook her head 'No.'

Another vehicle drove up. Two men seated by the fire got up and as they rose, they picked up firearms. They walked over to the newcomers and touched them.

Then all the men left the fire one of them kicking it until its parts, smoking and glowing in the gloom, subsided.

Each man walked slowly over to her. She was helped down by the driver. Each man bowed his head and shook her hand. Then one, an elderly man with glasses and a grim face, gently touched her in the small of her back. She understood and ran stumbling in the night to One Star.

The men quietly got into their vehicles. They ignored me. *Who* I wonder *set off my car ? Aren't we one people* I ask myself? This peninsula of sand glaring across the straits, is it truly separate from its counterpart over the water? The dhows since time immemorial plied their way in and out of Arabia, backwards and forwards leaving behind people, fabric, tea, ideas. The Arabs swarmed in the other direction carrying swords, the Koran, and latterly some fridge freezers. They created a great religion; then divided it. Yet are one. And what about us? Perfidious Albion. Colonising and extracting. Are we their brothers and sisters? I didn't think so. Someone has written me off. The Ruler?

The children must be left unscathed. I respect no ideology that does not hold children sacrosanct.

Like a captain I stand on the prow of this tectonic plate we sail into Eurasia and push up the Zagros Mountains as we go.

We are tectonically different. Iran champions the Shi'ite, downtrodden and subjugated in Arabia proper. They direct Hamas, support Assad, get behind Hizbullah, infiltrate Lebanon, work with the Houthis.

Iran gave much to Islam in mysticism and the Sufi. Unlike the Wahhabis. So different. Both have religious police. Iran's Heath Robinson democracy, does not suit the West for it is subordinate to the word of God. But when all is said and done Iran and Saudi hate each other. That is the physical reality. Hatred. And America has taken sides. To me this is a body blow.

Two percent of the Iranian population is Arab, so they say. But in the Emirates, there are as many people of Iranian extraction as the indigenous Arabs. Ethnically different. On this side there is ambivalence everywhere. Money disguises treachery. *And I am beginning to think America's blind spot is this.* Money that by passes hearts. And I? Here I sit, an expatriate from a nation that left its imprint upon history. Not loved. I am suspicious of dictators but employed by one. Without a gunboat to call up this seems a necessary arrangement if I am to do my thing. What do I treasure here? The Moon, the monsoon, the Tinah saline lagoon, flamingos, turtles, mangroves, and ospreys, maroon sunsets, the kharshaf cardoon and an Arab steed at 5.00 am on a bit and bradoon, and a swoon at noon.

And when I am bored, I read the story of the mares of King Mihrjan which are tethered by the shore at new moon tide to lure the stallions of the deep to break out of the surf and mount the mares, to breed the most beautiful horses in the world. I am anxious. Anxious that war and peace are decided by inexperienced and foolish people, who try to set an agenda clearly beyond them; and appear to connive at the unforgiveable. The beneficiary is China.

CHAPTER EIGHT

Next day, to my displeasure, my brother turned up like a bad penny, bringing bad luck.

'Sir, before your brother gets here,' said One Star, 'a guy rang up two or three days ago from Jeddah. Claimed to be a mate of yours. Says he is called haji al jallili or something like that. Wants to drop by and chew the fat. Sorry I forgot.'

'Oh dear, oh dear. No matter. Don't know what he wants?'

'He's something to do with the police.'

As soon as the man walked in, I knew he was on the cadge. Turned out he wanted a cheap hotel room.

'You should have phoned me,' I said.

He was very nicely turned out. His dishdasha immaculately clean looked as if it had a very, very light rinse of blue.

'I'm just hard up,' he said.

'Sorry to hear that.'

'Yes. I've sort of come off the payroll of the religious police. Or to be more exact most of the duties have been abolished. It's the Crown Prince you know? He has a new agenda. Football.'

'Well have a coffee. Tell me about yourself.'

He was middle aged, good looking, and his features neat and composed as if they had been very gently massaged with oil, olive oil?

'We met once,' he said. 'Of course.'

'Ah you remember. Do you remember my situation?'

'Not recently.'

'I was put in jail briefly for what they chose to call an honour killing. Anyone else would have been let off. But not me. No, not me.'

'Sorry to hear that.'

'So, I did a deal. I learned even more of the Koran than I already knew in exchange for a job. This troubled them. A devout man like me not being let off for an honour killing. Technically speaking.'

'How would that go down nowadays since the Crown Prince has changed things?'

'That's the problem. Everything has changed. The job I got was muhtasib. Because I knew the Koran backwards, I was qualified to police behaviours such as offending the holy book. Especially in schools. Now it's all changed. Guess what?'

'What?'

'Now they are going to teach music, theatre, art, evolution. Evolution! In school of all places. And as they loosen the influence of religion, they are letting women stand in municipal elections. A double whammy. What are we to police now?'

'Good point,' I said.

'Sharia is there to protect virtue. They will need me, eventually. But just for the moment I'm not exactly flush with cash. Can you help?'

'Inshallah. My secretary will talk to you. But what will you do now?

'I don't know. In the old days I would catch people trying to buy groceries during the time of prayer. But that is all done away with now. They keep changing the rules. But some things won't change. Mark my words.'

'I suppose so.'

They are talking about introducing a family law whatever that is. And human rights. Why? Because the Government is owned by America. Don't get me wrong: the Government is well meaning. But it has enemies.'

'No!'

'Yes. Next they will pretend to introduce democracy, an opposition, , freedom of speech. As if Americans practise human rights. Then the Qataris and the Shias will be laughing.'

'Some things never change. What did you have in mind?'

'Sharia. The family is the kernel of life. The State has to protect the family. And that means protecting fathers and husbands. Sharia does it. And then they will need not just the police, but good people to enforce it. People like me. What won't change is the Koran. That's where Khashoggi got it wrong. Some things are not negotiable.'

'There are many good people,' I said, 'but long ago it broke apart. After the death of the Prophet the Ridda wars started.'

'Not really. That's my point. In the beginning it was simple. We believe in God, in the Koran, in resurrection and the last judgement. But then the lawyers step in. More laws, less obedience. More laws, more deviousness. The laws become stricter. They forbid freedoms. So now they think more laws will make people free? No way. Borrow laws from the West? Don't go there; don't go there. If you do there will be war. It's in the Koran, isn't it?'

'You sound like a freethinker in the best sense; like a good Muslim confronted by the atheists, the heretics, even the Manicheans. The problems are not new. I have heard it said the apostasy laws were created and are still used to defend power. That Mahdi persecuted and executed freethinkers. Didn't he? From then on, atheists, materialists, even Sufi, were accused, even executed?'

'Not really. Yes, the law was enforced, and the problem became rare, you see?' he exclaimed triumphantly. Then his face dropped. 'We are betraying the book. No one is allowed to cite it if there is a suggestion of criticism of the regime.'

'Some people criticised Ali for not making war after the prophet died?'

'Well, that's how it was then.'

'I have heard in the Ottoman time the pressures to convert Christians led to new recruits recanting, saying it was all under duress and they didn't really mean it, so this led to massacres. People forget.'

'That is not going to happen,' he said firmly.

I got up.

'It has been a delight talking with you, I am sure you will be called again to defend the faith and support the Crown Prince. God bless you.'

In my spare time I found myself thinking more and more about my betrayal of Amelia. *In my whole life nothing,* I thought, *is more shameful than cowardice. What happened to me?* I asked myself. I remembered the line 'Be ready for me.' My insecurity returns.

Just when I didn't need it my brother came in waving a bottle of port.

'Hullo bro,' he cried. 'Have a bottle of Quarles Harris 1977. You deserve it. Brought it in my luggage. No probs.'

'You shouldn't have. You know port doesn't agree with me. Still, you're very welcome,' I said. 'Why don't I make you a cup of chai?'

And so we stretched ourselves out on the balcony and gazed at the mosque two streets away.

'How is your dear wife?'

'As dense as ever. Our marriage was based on a false prospectus.'

'How so?'

'She accused me of refusing to work; of unreasonable behaviour.'

'And your response?'

'This was followed by argument, evasion then further charges. For that reason alone, I refuse mediation. I will not be drawn into negotiating one lie after another. Time to stand up for myself.'

'That may be unwise. Get a mediator.'

'That's typical. When I got back from Africa, the family refused to include us in dinner parties. No wonder she dumped me. You could have stepped in, bro. But nowadays mediators mediate by balancing opposing positions. Then they big up the woman's side. The modern paradigm is seventy per cent of divorces are started by women. Seventy per cent of divorced women blame the menopause. Seventy per cent of women fall out of love well before their husbands. Reproduction in the

West is at issue. Men only win if they don't marry. Divorcing women should take a menopausal MOT and have their settlement reduced accordingly.'

'What does your solicitor advise?'

'She says we have a case against my wife based on cruelty. She thinks my wife is trapped in a psychopathia called narcissism.'

'Surely not.'

'She picked up Polly from hospital and threw her out of the car, when she was at her most vulnerable.'

'Sounds as if there are two sides to the argument.'

And so, the conversation circled until I was dizzy.

Where had it all gone so wrong?

From the first days of his marriage the klaxon signalled that a race had started to divide assets, past and future. Perhaps he absented himself too much. He had some business in Ghana selling wax prints to the fashion industry. The Ghanaians have a sophisticated market with yearly shifts in design. His partners, Chinese, were very demanding so he was always shooting off, planning and marketing.

'Did you ever take your wife with you?' I asked.

'Never. She did not understand. Things are difficult in Ghana,' he said. 'The Chinese gave them more credit than they can handle. I'm thinking of pulling out.'

'Maybe the pressure is getting to you. Talk to her,' I said.

'No. It's too late. She's menopausal.'

'Then get some support for her.'

'It goes back too far. Long ago she decided my family did not welcome her, so she began to plan a profitable withdrawal.'

'Were you in love?'

'Not now we're not.'

'Did you discuss this?'

'She doesn't believe in discussion. She sees everything as her process, in which her temper is supreme. The plot is well rehearsed. There is nothing wrong with divorce,' he said 'provided there is respect, but the modern way recognises only material reapportionment. Without *blame*, lies are free.'

'From the whistle she followed me around the house reciting the vostrum: everything you have and shall have is half mine. In an era of equality this may sound unexceptionable, but from day one no expression of love. As if love infringes equality.'

I took to wondering how I would I have fared with Amelia? Then I thought, I am a coward. That is my Achilles heel. My default was cowardice. But taking a page out of my professional playbook I reviewed progress in getting inside my brother's head. I failed because the treacle which passes for grey matter bogs me down. What is he? Just let me have a peep.

'Everything my wife says to my face she has leaked to an ever-widening circle,' he moans. 'First, she went to our son and daughters laying out her case. Next to the gardener and the char lady. Then to the wider circus.

The gardener and the char lady agree with her, not because she pays them, of course, but because they are her only friends.'

'Badmouthing your wife is unlikely to win support,' I said. 'Just think of the women trapped and bombed in Iraq, in Syria, in Israel, and Judea.'

'Have *you* got a girl friend?' he asked.

I chose not to mention Mrs Goldiwallah.

'Do you know what?' he said. 'I am going to fix you up.'

'Fix me up?'

'Yes. Find Mrs Irresistible for you.'

It doesn't work like that. Not for me, I thought.

But I said 'Oh, that's awfully kind.'

He is a weak man. I despise him.

I had a little drinks party. I invited the Wing Commander and his wife Shelley, MacSpity and Barbara, and Mr and Mrs Goldiwallah.

It was not a great success. I had put no thought into it.

It was a clash of cultures. The Wing Commander makes out he is superior to everyone else but is just a horse of a different colour. I feel vulnerable under his gaze. He does not know my history with his ex-wife. MacSpity stereotypes him as another here today gone tomorrow expatriate.

The powder keg turned out to be America aligned with Israel. The Wingco tests loyalties. America is Britain's oldest ally, he says; they saved us in the war.

MacSpity says the US attachment to Saudi and Israel is profoundly misguided. Israel actually *is* an American colony, he says, presumably quoting One Star.

'No,' I said. 'China is changing the game. They want to siphon off Saudi and Iran. I hope to see Islam unified.'

'No chance.'

'The Chinese propose a pharma JV with the Iranians,' I countered. 'I think Iran could be up for it.'

'We won't allow it,' said the Wing Commander. 'We'll see to that. We will make them back down.'

'One Star says China will create a rival to the WTO.'

'The problem is global warming,' said Goldiwallah. 'The Europeans are up in arms because the barometer got up to 45. That is nothing. The Europeans think nobody works in such temperatures. I have a message for them. Industrialisation is gonna move here. If the temperature is fifty we have the labour for it. They will work nights.'

'Who?'

'From the subcontinent.'

'You have to be joking,' said MacSpity.

'No, no,' said Goldiwallah.

'You hate material things, don't you Goldiwallah?'

'True.' As a matter of principle we don't buy second hand things, 'We feel the pain of the previous owner in parting with such things. It remains in the object itself even after you have bought it. We refuse to let this pain, this bitterness enter our lives.'

'What a wonderful and truthful refutation of materialism,' I said.

'You should read Avicenna', said Goldiwallah, obviously gratified. 'He contributed to our understanding of psychology. He coined the term for being possessed.'

'What kind of possession?' asked the Wing Commander sharply.

'Djinns,' said MacSpity.

'Made of smokeless fire,' said Goldiwallah.

'Remind me,' interjected the Wing Commander, 'about Djinns?'

'They are born as are we,' said Morgiana. 'They fall in love, get married and die. Some fly, some move mountains, some become visible at will. Some have goats' hooves and black tails.'

Goldiwallah interrupted trying to lighten the conversation. 'I have read that back in the day amulets of peony were a form of medicine,' he said.

'Nonsense,' said his wife. 'Before Islam the public were ignorant of medicine. Yet by the ninth century there was a hospital for the mentally ill in Baghdad.'

'But I respect my husband,' she said. 'Could he tell us what the word Mirgi refers to?' And she took his hand. I watched his face.

'Mirgi? Small death,' he replied. 'Its what they call epilepsy. It is completely curable in Pakistan, which is at the forefront of medicine in the region.' And he said this with a look of real pride.

'Is it a convulsion?'

'In Africa it is caused by worms in the head. In Nigeria it is contagious.'

'What is?'

'Mirgi. It is a psychiatric disease in Pakistan and Saudi. Some people think it is possession by parasites. In Mughal, India it was thought to be caused by nerves in the brain getting blocked.'

This all proved too much for the Wing Commander. He fixed Mrs Goldiwallah with a hostile gaze. 'If you are talking about what I think you are talking about, the West cracked it long ago.'

'Do tell.'

'This has yet to be fully validated, but microbes. Also tiny fragments in the brain. A seizure may well be a spasm which can reconfigure dystopia. I am speaking as a layman of course, but have firsthand experience.' He said this so loudly and with such vehemence no further comments were forthcoming.

Mr Goldiwallah broke the silence. 'Ever since Nasser, America pushed Europe out of it. Speaking as a Saudi I am confident the Crown Prince and the Americans see eye to eye.'

'Speaking as a Brit,' said MacSpity, 'we lost it in Iraq. Now Iran calls the shots. They prefer weak Presidents and glib Prime Ministers.'

It was the drink talking.

'But we both have democracy,' said the Wing Commander.

'The West ignore the majority. They have control. This fuels anarchy,' said MacSpity.

As the evening wore on the stress levels elevated.

'I read recently that flushing, sweating, palpitations, incontinence and sexual arousal are products of brain disease,' I said quietly to Mrs G.

'They are symptoms of love, a more dangerous condition,' she whispered.

'In my case,' I replied, 'males unaccustomed to love indulge in nose wiping, fidgeting, nail chewing, and blinking.'

'It is so.' She was having problems repressing laughter. 'By the way,' she said, 'keep a close eye on the Wing Commander. He is up to no good according to my husband. He's not your friend. I can't say more.'

'He has the holy disease. Mean anything?

'Certainly does. Google it. Could pay you handsomely.'

MacSpity announced loudly: 'I no longer trust expatriates.'

The Wing Commander was affronted. 'Why?' he demanded.

'No moral compass,' replied MacSpity.

'A rules-based order depends on America,' said the Wing Commander. 'That means aligning our interests on theirs. Europe went soft under Merkel. Now they're repatriating immigrants. What a shower. Socialism gives people what they want, which is a disaster. American democracy cuts out socialism to protect Americans but also Europe providing trading terms apply.

Mrs Goldiwallah intervened. 'We all share the same beliefs,' she said.

'No, we don't,' replied MacSpity. 'If there is peace across the Islamic world America will be the loser. Russia and China will then carve up the Middle East and Africa.'

'Three years ago,' the Wing Commander said, 'everything was calm. Then came Covid. Now the world order is teetering. Disease and the cost of limiting global warming changes everything. It is the era of migrants. The EEC can't cope. It amuses me when their media attack populists. Populism means the majority in Europe have ceased obeying the few who try to force feed the masses their leftist version of Liberal democracy, which is by definition, amoral.'

'I believe People cannot be moral and free at the same time. The core tenet of the European democrat is untrue. I believe in a humanity created by God, so my belief means we are never free. The commandments curtail freedom.'

'The Quran trumps the earlier versions,' said Mr Goldiwallah. 'The story goes that God created the Earth, and then humans. He appointed humans as stewards of the Earth. The Angels were surprised. Humans, they said, are corrupt and violent. God replies: I know things you do not know. Humans have free will. You Angels do not. They were flummoxed.'

'That doesn't compute,' said MacSpity. 'To avoid sin mankind always exercised free will.'

'And are never free,' chimed the Wing Commander.

'All of us know creation,' repeated Goldiwallah. 'We are one culture.'

I decided to calm the waters.

'You are right,' I said. 'Christian belief is still the bedrock of the Western alliance. Of course humans get things wrong. But one thing we can agree on: the role of each unique human in redemption; our task is to redeem ourselves. And Nature,' I added.

The Wing Commander rolled his eyes.

'In Islam God created a tree of immortality,' MacSpity explained. 'In the Bible it was a tree of knowledge. It's not the same you know. Satan refused to bow to Adam, because, he said, "I am fire and spirit and I do not bow to something made of dirt."'

'The problem is American ignorance,' he said. 'The worst thing that ever happened was the fall of communism. It ushered in naked economic power, mad individualism and degeneracy unleashed in American culture, which is based on greed. When the Chinese take over where will they turn for guidance?'

'America,' said the Wing Commander, 'thank God. A word of advice. Stay away from Oman.' This was addressed at me.

'I've already picked up advice along those lines', I replied. 'If you know something I don't know you should say so.'

'There are contracts out, so I hear.'

At the end of the evening MacSpity had difficulty walking. At one point he appeared to be getting on with Mrs Goldiwallah, whispering to her behind his hand as if they were playing tennis.

The Wing Commander frowned. MacSpity uncharacter-istically looked frightened. 'I have lived here all my life,' he said, and I do not remember having this sensation, that I am a total foreigner here.'

'In your own country?' I asked ironically.

'Don't you start,' he replied, and stiffened like an ironing board.

On his departure he turned to Barbara. 'I will find a lady for this man. He is the only sane person here.'

I was sorry One Star was being attacked behind his back. The most important aspect of love is pity. If you cannot bear to lose someone, then you feel the desperate need to protect them. This feeling of protective love raises the beloved to something wonderful.

One Star is part of me. His absence would be unbearable. It would be an exaggeration to say I love him. I don't want to exaggerate. But in a way he is my alter ego. You only have to hear him tell children's stories to know he reads my mind. What is unforgiveable is I feel for him what I cannot feel for Amelia.

CHAPTER NINE

Amelia is incomprehensible for a start.

I sometimes think there is a secret protocol requiring women to seek out men programmed to surrender, transfixed like unicorns, sequestered and disarmed. I never know what she thinks of me.

Her marriage broke up ages ago.

When I first came out here, air conditioning was not great. Amelia would have found it intolerable. She would have insisted on returning to England immediately.

If she and I had walked together on the beach, and watched the long low silhouettes of the great tankers on the horizon, we could have found love listening to the sound of the shamal, as it reflects the gentler softer sounds of the sea. We could have watched the sheen of water, centimetre or two deep, lighting the placid sands.

And at sunrise, together we would have listened to the call to prayer and I would have taught her how God makes the sky glow as it enfolds the brightening shadows.

We would have greeted each other at dawn when the carapace of stars wheels into eternity.

This is the Near East the birthplace of stars, and of religion.

And then dimly I become aware of the choices I would have faced. *Would I return to one who I once was when everything was possible*? Have I closed down the promise of my young years? Did my hopes switch off forever? Does the best in us survive somewhere in time; or will the real me merely evaporate? Can I wipe the past clean? Can I make my life must I submit to my free will it in all its errors?

I thought of the great love of poetry in this region and in Europe when the two cultures interlocked. Chretien de Troyes gave expression to chivalry, in its day a beautiful idea entailing piety and selflessness yet bound by romantic love, and Christianity, wrought in words as hard as enamel to express the infinite.

Yet such ideas break and disperse upon Amelia as sea breaks on the foreland.

Can love be infinite? Not at all. I felt sad. She is ephemeral but has such power over me I am at a loss. I do not understand her. But trying to persuade her to open up I feel excited sexually.

Is love as some seem to believe, an oxymoron somewhere between commitment, and humiliation? Between rejection and domination.

Falling in love is, I thought, *similar to what happens in the anterior* Insula. The Insula is part of the brain according to Amelia which predicts what will happen next. Then our senses report back what is actually going on in the big wide world. If the Insula is surprised by the result, it summons blood and then either changes the prediction, or the world outside. An aura invokes the calm before the electrical storm which bursts upon the brain. For a brief moment all becomes clear and certain. Ecstasy is felt. The mind opens. Then the storm breaks.

In love the same certainty is felt. The beloved coincides with expectation. A voice speaks. Instead of an electrical storm the mind is enthralled; the body acts. The anterior Insula dwells on the subjective: intense worship follows.

What happened on the road to Tarsus when God came upon Paul?

In religion the physical world changes to match the spiritual. The Grail was wrought from the Dome of the Rock, holy both to Judaism, Islam, and Christianity.

Does true belief have to be the property of one religion over another? Mrs Goldiwallah came up with a solecism. 'Someone,' she said, 'has written: "God has no form, no shape, no colour, no differences, no race, no religion, no country, no place, no name, neither beginning nor end."

'He is vanishingly superior,' I replied.

'He was made to worship,' said Mrs Goldiwallah.

'Made? A tall order. He is elusive.' I replied.

'He?' she asked. 'I thought you were attached to Ambaji?'

Later I comforted myself. Belief is inspiration. Across a great tapestry of glittering mosques and brilliant madrassahs, ornamented with a kaleidoscope of greens and blacks and reds, geometry in love with beauty pays homage. And is there not one ultimate heaven beyond all these holy places and all these beliefs? But the poetry and the delicious Persian cartoons on love and the green smoke, and the green eyes of their jinniyah all contribute to creativity of those born under this sky. I reflected on the Wing Commander's suggestion that a seizure may like a sneeze, be a convulsion intended to clear the mind.

I called on Amelia in my official capacity. 'I am in security working for the Ruler,' I said. 'My job entails collecting information about visitors to the territory, so regrettably …

'If you must.'

She looked her most narcissistic, as if above questioning.

'All part of my job,' I said. She watched me with beautiful, resentful eyes.

'I am required to ask of you, formally. You know. What are you doing here? What is your relationship with the Iranians? What formal exchange of letters, emails, and contracts do you have with them?'

'Nothing,' she said brusquely. 'None.'

'The Iranians don't like being pissed about. I can be helpful to you.'

'Maybe,' she said stonily.'

'One minute you can, the next minute you can't. But if they must be hostile they will suffer…'

'The Iranians have an astonishing capacity to suffer and a culture of great depth, subtlety; and resilience. They are open to Western propositions offered on equal terms'

'So please respond formally to the following: the purpose of your visit; contacts in the territory that may have consequences for their institutions and finances and yours.'

Angry at the outset she remained so. 'Where is my right to privacy?' she demanded. 'Who interferes with my freedom to talk to Iran?'

'You have no right unless we so decide,' I replied. 'Last time we spoke I talked about the *extraordinary limen* here between two competing powers culturally, religiously militarily. They stand firm against enemies, as we always did. Were we wrong to stand against hostile powers? France, Spain, then Germany. Iran too stands against Britain and America. The recent slaughter has shocked them. If you want my advice, steer clear.'

'My science demands the opposite!'

'This stretch of water flows between life and death. On the one hand the Western powers and Sunni Arabia, which seems apply for membership. On the other, Iran in alliance with Alawites and Shia,and some say, the Chinese.'

'So why do they cross swords with Pakistan?'

'Terrorists. They have taken up residence everywhere. Their productivity has so far been modest. I assume you are like me in the American camp?'

'Science does not take sides.'

'I insist on being told your plans: whom you intend to meet, when you propose to travel and how. Your word alone will not do. I must see the documents.'

'Well, this is a surprise,' she replied. 'I have very confidential information which I shall not share with you.'

'I will interview your superior.'

'My research project is supervised, examined and technically reviewed at the appropriate level.'

'And what is the subject of your project?'

'Medicine.'

'Well, perhaps you would help me. What field of medicine?'

'Immunology.'

'Some kind of breakthrough?' While I did not confide in Amelia I am well aware that spying is, in part, the business of preventing the other side from winning. If the Professor were to deny the Iranians his science this puts me at a disadvantage ethically

'Professor Hughes Hallett is the man to speak to,' said Amelia. 'I am travelling with him to Al Buraimi to meet associates.'

'I too am heading that way. Perhaps the three of us could meet there? If I leave these forms with you, it would be helpful if you were to fill in the appropriate sections.'

'I hate you,' she said.

Maybe, I thought, *I can steal a march. I could lead her to believe we can penetrate the labyrinth of Teheran. What does Hughes Hallett want, I wonder? A middleman?*

When I caught up with them in Buraimi, I could see Science had strayed into dangerous geography.

'Our work is extremely confidential and subject to UN oversight,' said Hughes Hallett.

'My forms are pure bureaucracy,' I said apologetically. Still, if you wouldn't mind... Is your work funded by Britain?'

'No,' he said amiably, 'but by America, disproportionately. There are enclaves of young men over there whose life expectancy is half their counter parts' in Brazil even Ethiopia. The difference is due to inequality. Our work will alleviate this. It can help the problem in the West Bank, which is catastrophic. It's simply not possible to get you up to speed. Don't know why I am bothering. But hey listen up. Disease and malnutrition feed off deprivation. The genome is key. Microbes, and substances they secrete into blood vessels, travel directly to the brain and talk to the brain.

'Microbes resist pathogens, control inflammation and improve immune response. Microbes shape diet, even if it is made worse by marketing.

'Microbes prompt neuropod cells in the gut lining to stimulate the vagus nerve, which connects directly to the brain.

'Microbes activate enteroendocrine cells. Hormones influence mood, and well being.

We are confident of our ability to control microbes.'

'Our intellectual property, involves protocols and research on the following:

Metabolism, immune systems, and behaviours; Enzymes e.g. promoting storage of adipocytes; biochemical pathways that store fats in liver and muscles.'

I really did not understand. Instinctively I thought to myself: *this is all bullshit. Something more scary is afoot. I must insist on fairplay.*

Hughes Hallett went on 'We can activate and suppress immune systems inducing recovery, torpor, and death, to order.'

I frowned and closed my eyes momentarily, then tried winging it. 'It sounds from an ethical point of view, a bit aggressive,' I said.

Hughes Hallett smiled.

'Do you intend to manipulate immune systems to scale?'

'Don't talk to me about morality,' he said. 'We have technology which can be sold at high margins in the West. But our aim is to restore health in Africa and the Middle East and so undo the harm caused by the developed world.

'Just one of our low value-added products increases survival among the malnourished by better use of waste materials. Just think the big picture. What if we maximise nutrition from things no-one eats?'

'But,' I said, 'if Governments get your intellectual property, couldn't this be turned on its head? Biological warfare?'

'Leave risk assessment to the experts. We factor in that sort of thing at the next stage. We might throw in enhanced fertility. We have a treasury in the pipeline. We just need support from Governments. The UN are behind us. It is the future. I am about to go into meetings with Saudi scientists. I want to meet Iranian equivalents. We have made contacts but not the right ones,' he said. 'If you have any suggestions please let us know.

'OK,' I said. 'I'll give it a shot.' But I thought he is either a saint or dreadfully naïve.

I took a nap and dreamed again. This time an aircraft carrier the length of Oxford Street swept through the straits and demolished Fujeirah. A fleet of dhows hemmed it in, reinforced by enormous junks. Completely surrounded, seamen descended from the carrier and swarmed over the dhows.

Surgeons in immaculate white came on deck, but ran inside again.

I agreed to meet up with Amelia at 6.00 o'clock.

At the bar I bought her an Alvear PX, ice cold. 'You have been busy with the old bunsen burner,' I said. 'Hope you get the credit.'

'Don't worry. He has a terminal illness, she said. 'Off the record.'

'Good Lord. Then what's he doing out here?'

'He is obsessive. I can manage. I have just finished rereading the Second Sex. I admire Simone de Beauvoir; you know? Do you think I would run the gauntlet without her? Men jeering and making blue jokes, and pushing me around?'

'Got you going, has she?'

'No, but feminism works for me.'

'And Marxism?'

She looked blank, mad as a hatter. I was in love again.

Three Saudis came in with Hughes Hallett; he introduced them and mumbled something about me. The Saudis looked disinterested. They headed off leaving Amelia and me to finish our drinks.

Why did she back out all those years ago? But just then One Star appeared. He was dressed smartly in a Western suit, but his face seemed swollen. He had been drinking.

'One Star! Good to see you,' I said insincerely, as his presence could get us into trouble.

'Are you going to introduce me?' he asked, his voice thick with drink.

'Let me introduce Amelia, whose itinerary you arranged.'

'Delighted.'

'Good to meet, said Amelia.

'I think you know Dylan from way back,' he countered. 'You are fortunate.'

'You think so?

He put one hand on the bar to steady himself.

'Dylan taught me everything I know, he said.

'Which is?'

I interrupted. 'One Star thinks the Germans and the Russians are destined to be allies. He says they have already reached an understanding.

I said this unfairly to put him in his place.

'I don't remember that,' he said. 'This world survives if nations collaborate and put the natural world back together again.'

'How original,' said Amelia! 'You mean the entropy of the isolated system? Like Humpty Dumpty?'

'The subtest,' he replied obscurely. The subtest is that the most dynamic nations will leave the institutes America owns: UN

IMF, World Bank, WTO, ICJ; and create ones they prefer.'

'And who are these dynamic ones?' she asked tongue in cheek? 'What is it they have in common?'

'All capable of independence and innovation: BRICS but more so. India, Brazil, Indonesia, Nigeria. Even Iran. Congo. All different. All destined to grow in a world no longer American.'

'No China? No Russia?'

'China is the catalyst. They have followers, or in a sense colleagues. Russia for one. Some hate America. I have in mind South Africa, Pakistan, Yemen, Afghanistan.'

'How lovely,' said Amelia. 'Is there a board game we may play?'

To my horror his eyes filled with tears, and falling to his knees with both hands he took hold of my right shoe.

'You are my guru', he said. 'I have erred, he said.

To my shame I found this unacceptable. It was as if his ramblings were somehow mine. He could not make a spectacle of me like this.

What was worse a scientist who was there to consult with Amelia, witnessed his anti-American tirade.

One Star leaped up and ran to the lift.

Amelia turned to me, eyes ablaze.

'Do you trust him?' she demanded. 'You were once infatuated with me, as this man is with you. I don't like it. I think you do.'

'I do not.'

This seemed to calm her.

'I have more serious things to think about,' she said. 'Forget about your Assistant and his curious ideas. Autoimmune mediated disease as an etiology became a thing thirty years ago when new brain antibodies were being discovered. Patients with autoimmune diseases were found to have higher risk. That's when I made my mark. Ten percent of people suffering from stiff persons syndrome go on to develop problems, sometimes triggered by viral encephalitis. Diagnosis is difficult not least because the exact causes of autoimmune disorders were unknown until I came by.

That was Amelia to a T.

I spoke to Esa.

'I think I know now what they have got', he said.

'What?'

'Have you heard of the holy disease?'

'No.'

'I think they have a way to spread it.'

'Then others will be working on it too,' I said sarcastically. 'If you want to get in on this you will have to stop playing silly buggers and work through me. No more arrests. No more blackmail.'

'That is IRGC. I have no influence.'

'Then forget it.'

'We can't do that.'

'Western science is sublime. You are out of your league, Esa.'

'We have the answer. Hybrid war. You will not know until it hits you.'

'Do you want Amelia's help or not?'

'Maybe. Disease is not uncommon here. We have good people.'

'Who?'

'Pasteur Institute.'

I laughed.

'I will get top man Velayat-e Faqih on the case.'

'In the meantime I will get little Amelia to speak to you.'

'Why not bring her over to us?'

'We distrust you.'

He held my upper arm tightly.

'You loved her? Once?' he asked impertinently.

'But Esa, I love you too. I have lived close to you. Islam itself means nothing to me personally, just as Christianity, misused or abused, does not mean much to me either. But I love God and your history as God fearing people. Your people created a great culture. You deserve to have this science. Support me and I will put Amelia in your hands.'

'That's good. Did you hear the gunshots outside your hotel last night?'

'No?'

'They must have told you. Your Personal Assistant was shot dead.'

'What? What? No! No! No!'

'Someone took exception to his politics.'

'What a pity. I thought he was on to something,' said Amelia when I told her. I don't see why symbiosis can't be the watch-word of statesmen as well as science.'

'I know nothing of such things. This is your subject. We British and the Americans hold our noses frightened of Islamophobia.'

'Poor little boys frightened of fear. Science defines terms and tests them. It is more grown up than you.'

None of this would bring One Star back.

Amelia retreated into neurology. She talked randomly about near death experience and impaired consciousness during seizures. An aura, peculiar to each individual, leads to changes in perception; how objects look taste, smell, feel; or purvey ecstasy.

She drew my attention to the role her supervisor plays when investigating brain disease. Apparently he finds which part of the brain connects to near death experiences. He reports that neurosurgeons can stimulate the Insula to induce ecstasy. Amelia cannot accept that the divine is involved in the human brain. The Divine in near death experiences, which are necessarily rare means nothing to her.

I speculate that our brains have evolved to reach for these experiences because our biology has spiritual potential. Our subjective feelings reach naturally for the divine.

'It is impious to insert human love into this explanation, except that love at its most high and passionate will, I believe, include submission to God.'

'Rubbish,' says Amelia. This row relieved the pressure I was under after learning of One Star's death.

'But why should we be surprised if brain disease echoes our higher feelings,' I said. 'This has affected me extraordinarily. I feel One Star's loss as if I have lost a child. Death has galvanised me. From what I hear a near death experience invokes submission, when One Star's friends and dear ones gather round to mourn his passing.'

'These thoughts seemed to explain why mankind rarely experiences the divine directly. Prophetic visions of heaven and hell are not fantasies, but language and imagery embedded in biology.'

I consulted my I Phone. EEG recordings of NDE are reported to continue for up to 15 minutes before and after death. When researchers focus on the 30 seconds before and 30 seconds after death, they observe changes in wave patterns like those in people dreaming. This raises fascinating questions about the source and purpose of such dreams. A replay of memories and visions of our lives before we die is in fact a record of self-knowledge at the meeting with our maker.

Of course I dare not confess this to Amelia, least of all now. Her presence and her very character daze me. Under pressure I see it is loyalty which binds me to her. She says she will help me. If she commits, she will be one hundred per cent loyal, but practical, without thought of souls or of eternity.

I asked her to fix a meeting with Roy. They came.

'You want me to introduce you to influencers?' I reminded them.

'You said you would investigate?'

'Should there be any kind of transaction or commercial advantage, my employer will want to know what he is getting out of it.'

'I can assure you there won't be anything like that,' said Hughes Hallett. 'We're not commercially driven. We are altruists. As such we favour partners who play by the rules, our playbook, our ethical standards.'

'Not here you won't.'

'Salazar, Franco are outside our circle,' Amelia said tartly.

'This is not a beauty contest,' I replied. 'There is a peaceful way to better government. In Europe there are lots of countries unpractised in such arts. They think democracy is to do with Presidents.'

'Sorry, but I can't offer your employer a false prospectus,' said Amelia.

'If your intellectual property is the difference between life and death, you may be a sitting duck.

'We are very well regarded in the UN, in WHO, and in America.'

'None of that will help round here.'

'Meaning?'

'Just that. This region is a hotbed of conspiracies, feuds, religious passions. It's like the old-style Balkans. Well organised militias, fanatics armed and trained, weak statelets ripe for overthrow, great powers energetically manoeuvring behind cover, Third World countries overpopulated and economically weak, desperate for change, ready for dictatorship, fearful of invasion. And to put the cap on it we have neo-colonialism in Africa exported out of the Middle East. Have you run this past Israel? All I would say to you is: choose your partners well. Exclude everyone else. Don't offer it on licence. And, if you insist on going into Iran, let me organise it for you, better still come with you. I want you to come back in one piece.'

Hughes Hallett intervened with some authority. 'I must be frank,' he said. 'What we bring to the table is our ability to manage immunity. Immunity to what, you ask? In the areas under study, we have unearthed two major opportunities. At the geopolitical level it is dangerous if one politic has it and one does not. I admit it. We will inform you of the detail in due course. But will you and your employer help us to share our science not just with Saudi but Iran as well.'

'I think you must. I will consult with my employer.'

I rang Esa.

'Esa, old fruit. Have you had any dealings with this Hughes Hallett person?'

'Not yet.'

'Do you want to?'

'He seems unreal, boss. Possibly not of this world for long.'

'Quite. Let's just agree to cut him out of it.'

I like to joke that I am on the Sunni side of the street. The battle between the Saudis and the Iranians is part of a bigger problem. Neither are especially interested in starving Africans, let alone auto immunity. If they go for biological weapons, the Shias are numerous, and vulnerable. Iran is opportunist. Their link up with Russia fits with being nimble, evasive, trench shy, and expert in hybrid strategies against America. Trump reneged on their negotiations on nuclear.

We might as well send Amelia to the Iranians. She will learn what we are up against. What had I got to lose? The IRGC might arrest her, and hold out for a swapsie or trade concessions. But with access to high grade science they may come down to earth.

Was I going to betray Amelia again? What is of no interest to her: religion, the human spirit; things which defy AI cannot be measured. To her scale is everything. The microbiota in their vast legions are, to her, real, in a way that God is not. Yet the end of the world will multiply fears of hell fire even amongst atheists. I am desperate to balance my new found passion with doing the right thing by Iran. My other passion is spying. Mrs G says the Wing Commander is up to no good, but refuses to say how. I must force it out of her. If Amelia is going to Iran, I will do my best to ensure her safety. First, she can meet Esa.

CHAPTER TEN

I am desperate to clear my mind and take a break. Mrs G has insights into the region's politics. And her husband has something on the Wing Commander. I must find out. After all, I am a spy. Am I on the right track? I decided to go down to the Oman with her. A luxury dhow was hired for the purpose.

The captain and his single crew member were asked politely not to interrupt us.

After we had stowed overnight things I chucked in a canvas, oil paints, and an easel.

We weighed anchor. Our badinage, shall we call it, washed over the crew without offending them. I got her to talk about her husband.

'There are reasons,' I said to her, 'why art becomes successful at one time and not another; and why art is neglected in some cultures.'

'Art,' she said, 'in my case, is cinema. In India and Pakistan, the movies are what move us. They are our window on the world. We have a growing middle class and the unnumbered poor, hungry for life. All love the movies. Bit like the UK in the Thirties. Maybe?'

'I wouldn't know. Your husband. Does he like cinema?'

'He just breaks up. *Sleepless in Seattle*? Wept like a baby. Embarrassing.'

'Could there be a cinema industry in the Gulf?'

'No, never. For one thing they've already wasted too much money. They pour it into the ground. It'll never happen. A successful home-grown cinema industry here on the coast. No way unless they follow Hollywood and completely despoil their culture. That picture '*Djinn*' was a disaster. In the end the talent was American, in other words riddled with untruth. Real culture in Arabia is often secretive, sometimes primal, hidden from intruding eyes. But Iran. 'There's the place for Cinema. Wonderful. Of course theirs is a very old civilisation, very rich, cosmopolitan, famous. They had theatre thousands of years ago. Ta'zieh Naqqali. They take to Cinema like ducks to water.'

She wiped three perfect pearls of sweat from her forehead. 'They go to Cannes and win prizes,' she said. 'For me Cinema shows who has culture. Not Britain! not in a fit! The subcontinent, Iran. Yes. That's the ticket.'

At this point I became animated and, nearly falling out of the boat,went down on my knees. Mrs G grabbed me and restored me to my feet.

After we separated arms, locks, and cameras, I suggested there may be other reasons for Iranian success. 'Do you believe in Djinns?' I asked.

"I know a bit about Africa and Pakistan. The spirit world and possession are common in both. Djinns are believed by most. My husband for one. You Westerners are unaware of this. You never look beneath the surface.'

'Now you know, my dear Mrs Goldiwallah, that I love painters and painting. Drawbacks round here are psychological and topographical.'

'I love Monet,' she said; lovely pink and blue cathedrals, beautiful as butterflies. But it is hard to imagine them winning here.'

'Impressionism is about light, not pastel shades,' I said.

'There's plenty of light here,' she waved at the glittering sea, and the bright, bright sky. 'It's free.' Her waving hands displayed freckles. *Irreverently I wondered if she had inherited genes from Alexander the Great, along with her undoubted valour.*

'But light kills colour,' I insisted. 'Down in the Oman where we will shortly take our pleasures, the Green Mountains are pure grey. The sun kills colouring, stone dead.'

'You can paint them green.'

'Very good. Very good. This is how art is of little consequence here. That and the good book. The strength of the sun stops serious painting. The breakthrough of Monet was light unlocking his pleine air landscapes.'

'Oh! I don't care a toss about plainer landscapes, excuse my Urdu. The French have had their day in painting. Even a Pakistani can tell you that.'

'Monet discovered how to make an envelope of light in his paintings. He created envelopes of light embracing the whole landscape and brought it to life. Imagine doing that here. Colour painted in the full light of a fervid day is drained away and poured down the mind's sink like tinted water after cooking a green vegetable.'

'Well, tell me which is your favourite film'

'Mine is *Giant*', said she. 'No I tell a lie; actually it is *Jawani Phir Nahi*. All-time great.'

'Mine is *Jules et Jim* or *L'Annee derniere a Marienbad*.'

'Never heard of it. I can tell from your accent they're French. I thought you Brits didn't go for French.'

'Quite the opposite. But they have seen better days. Like us. In 1870 the Germans gave the French a good pasting just when the Impressionists came out in open revolt. Traditional French painting then went on the skids, save for a couple of Spaniards. Sometimes you can tell a whole culture is going down the pan. Decadent. Then society goes into foment. Or decays. The French were decadent for a century.'

'At making war?'

'At art and philosophy. It's what happens. People get trapped in the past. Unless brave souls rebel, the culture dries up and implodes. The Germans never looked back. The French went soggy and Marxist and have yet to recover from Foucault.'

'You Europeans are funny; out of the Ark. Isn't that what you say?'

'We live in a dynamic world. The idea that a conversation between the art elite might have a counterpart in this neck of the woods is implausible. The tradition does not exist. Test your husband.'

'I wouldn't dare. He's not as soft as you are. But we have great thinkers who led the world,' said Mrs Goldiwallah proudly.

'So you did. But when Mohammad, blessed be his name, told us God created life did he not say that a depiction of man may tempt the viewer to worship the picture instead of God?'

'I don't know. Did he?'

'In Europe there were those who believed light to be an emanation from God; a fit subject for their art.'

'I don't know anything about that either.'

'I know what you're about to say,' I replied. 'Words in Islam are themselves art. They are a sufficiency for relaying the messages of God. Illustrations to accompany these words are gratuitous.'

'That is exactly what I was about to say.'

'Good girl. For some reason Italians such as Cimabue, Simone Martini, Giotto, Duccio felt illustration of the Gospels helped men to see. Perhaps their priests had mislaid the power of speech?'

'Ha, ha. No, it was because they did not have a magnificent language.'

'Exactly. And there followed in the European Renaissance visual art which brought to life the story of Christ from the deep past. I am in love with the subject of landscape painting. I know its history in Italy, France, and the Low Countries. Gombrich to me is like your Avicenna. Now come and sit beside me and we will gaze on the shores of these great lands, and I will describe the landscape of my dreams, and express them in my destitute and clumsy language.'

So we drank sherbert, and sang songs and I began to feel I was on holiday which now explained why I had decided to come. And we felt good towards each other, despite the crew.

'I am tempted to think England has always been provincial,' I remarked portentously. 'Add to this I am a show off; I think I can fool you by throwing about the names of artists you've never heard of.'

'I love you when you are pompous,' said Mrs Goldiwallah.

'In my own way I create anew a world of knowledge which mirrors my world of espionage. Now tell me what do you really know about the Wing Commander? Are you still refusing to tell me what your husband has on him?'

'You mean the plan which has been hatched to kill the Wing Commander,' she said, rather to my surprise.

'Do you know who lies behind this er... plan?'

'I do.'

I smiled and pronounced: When anarchy is afoot, abandon conventional thinking.'

She explained: 'He is in the pocket of the Americans, and the Israelis and plans to steal your Amelia's secrets and stop them leaking to Iran.'

'How will he do this?'

'Our intuition is guided by clues which have been liberally fed into the public sphere. A rumour is going the rounds, that he has not suffered a seizure causing him to collapse out jogging in the late afternoon. He did not get a black eye that day. On another occasion he is reported not to have bitten his tongue.'

'Either a disease, or someone wants us to think so,' I said.

'His own doctor says the Wing Commander has problems.'

'So I hear.'

'Perhaps you might look into a sudden disorderly expenditure of force throughout the body. I have one condition. You must find out his medical condition. My idea is that he has fits, and is possessed by a Djinn.'

'That does not sound like the Wing Commander. Is he taking medicine? Could you find that out for me?'

'I might,' she replied. 'I will. I have heard,' she added, 'that he has begun to vary his jogging routine to avoid desperadoes. But if he is possessed, he is the desperado.'

'So, he is up to no good. What does no good mean? I see him as a senior official devoted to the pax Americana. Am I wrong?

'Of course you're wrong, if he is possessed. I should watch your back. He has it in for you. Let's suppose he wants us to think he is in hospital at the exact moment he kidnaps Amelia.'

'What should we do?'

'Find out if he is recruiting GUAM special forces. In other words, Americans.'

'Do you think they can coerce Amelia?'

'I have heard they want to keep her science to themselves.'

'My instinct is to save her.'

'Me, too. Let's ask MacSpity for help,' said Mrs Goldiwallah. 'He likes you. He is tough. MacSpity has friends along the coast. You need to set a trap. Get word to the Wing Commander you plan to send Amelia to Iran. He won't like that. His plans will fall apart if she is delivered to the wrong address. Tell him to meet you at Ras al-Khaima.'

'What about Fujeirah?'

'No. Ras al-Khaimah. Give the Wing Commander the details of place and time. Get him to imagine she will be at his mercy.'

'Wouldn't you be better at sowing these seeds Mrs Goldiwallah? You met him at my drinks party. So it will be easy for you.'

'I'll think about it,' she replied. 'Talk to MacSpity.'

'The Wing Commander and MacSpity's mutual dislike may come in useful after all? Thank goodness I've got you on my side. You are a good girl. While we are in Oman, I intend to visit Bahla. Are you game?'

'I would be quite happy to visit Nizwa and look at the farm there. They have nice irrigation systems. You know the Omanis learned their irrigation from the Persians and their magnificent Falajs which suckle on the high bosom of the mountain and carry sweet water a thousand miles to a little field of alfa alfa in the desert.'

'A very ancient practice.'

'And did you know they hold an auction of that water and divert it to the highest bidder through little wooden trap doors in the falaj? Proto-capitalism.'

'Can we also visit Bahla? It has,' I explained, 'a long history of Djinn activity. There is much that I may learn.'

'Young beautiful women are believed to fall prey to Djinns in Pakistan,' said Mrs Goldiwallah. 'It makes sensational PR.'

'What is your explanation of a Djinn?'

'Their commander in chief is Iblis. He is not ranked highly in religion but is formidable.'

'Well, you should know Bahla is the home of Djinns and the fire associated with them. I have read how a Shaman there lures a Zar Djinn to possess someone who is ill. The Shaman then calls the Zar spirit to come forth and expels it from the possessed. What do you make of that?'

'Spooky,' said Mrs G. 'Sounds like a job for Djinn busters. Sometimes when the Angel of Death passes by, men suffer pains and sadness and see things like ghouls, and hear warning sounds like swarms of locusts. I have heard it said: be alarmed at the sound of the ringing bell, for that is the instrument of Satan. Or you will see the Angel of Death.'

'Have you ever experienced anything like that yourself?' I asked her. 'St Paul said it is better to marry than burn with passion.'

'I can vouch,' said Mrs G, 'for both. I believe in Djinns and medicine, both.'

And so we chugged down past Sohar and landed at Muttrah.

We registered at a passable hotel (not a Disney one in the Jebel Akhdar). Mrs Goldiwallah told me to look up brain disease on my phone, then subsequently began to snore ever so gently. So I studied diseases on the Wi-Fi. Seizures have been around for ever, said my iPhone. Do you not know? it said. Indian medicine, during the Vedic period included fits 3000 years ago.

In Ayurvedic literature of Charaka Samhita (which dates to 400 BC), seizures were described as 'apasmara' which means 'loss of consciousness'. Pass the smelling salts. It contains abundant references to symptomatology, aetiology, and treatment. To think they used such big words so long ago. I woke Mrs G. 'I have lots to report. Have you read Ayurvedic literature? Charaka Samhita?' 'No. I am wondering if they sell Nivea cream here?'

'Did you ever hear of Karen Armstrong?' I asked her.

'I did hear her sing once.'

'Not that one. Did you ever read a book by Suzanne O'Sullivan about symptoms? How difficult they are to find.'

'I did not,' she said. 'But I have heard the same thing about love.'

'Karen's neurologist taught her diseases suffered by religious people include visions of peace, joy, and significance.'

'Does that not sound like falling in love?'

'Are you in love, Morgiana?' I enquired and breathed into her ear.

'Not in the sense you mean. Please don't do that.'

'When she was 13, Joan, the feminist, was ecstatic imagining lights.

Other people talk of an aura which, like a cold breeze runs up your leg. Then a sense of delightful holiness. What can it mean?'

'Sounds uncomfortable.'

'Could it be this the Wing Commander has?'

'If he proposes to play a trick on us let's persuade him we have fallen for it. Show him we are taken in?' But Mrs G had left me in the lurch. All that remained was her gentle snore. I continued my research.

Modern scientists speculate that Ezekiel presented fainting spells. He had difficulty speaking, but not writing, a trait called hypergraphia. The *Book of Ezekiel* is the fourth longest in the Bible. Ezekiel and Tolstoy are considered religious, a characteristic associated reasonably enough with too much writing.

Had the Persians met Hippocrates halfway they might have uncovered another foundation stone to medicine. Two Greek tragedies, one about Iphigenia sacrificed by her father, a nasty patriarch, and another about Heracles by the playwright Euripides. They talked of the sacred disease, because it was thought, like eros, or love, to be visited on men by gods. Hippocrates probed the links to mental disorder. So what do gods mean here? Modern thinkers seem to interpret gods as ciphers that inform physics, biology, and even symbiosis, which underpin survival, evolution, extinction. As in much of their development, the Greeks combined cold reason with the explosive creativity of their art.

Certain kinds of love and violence were visited by gods often on great leaders equivalent in their way to Hitler and Stalin. Euripides shows Orestes after killing his mother, Clytemnestra. On the seashore he jerks his head violently up and down. He groans. His hands shake. He rushes about in a frenzy. A chorus links the sea to the disease. He falls to foaming. His pulse is gone.

Madness erupted in Heracles. Madness imposed by the gods. Greeks were ambivalent about this. In their terms the divine, and the medical were true at the same time.

Hippocrates thought the brain was open to disease. Symptoms suggested a border between human and divine, and the traffic across that border. The Greeks experimented on goats, the better to see the flow of blood into the goat's brain. Heracles suggests something in the body causes madness just as now we think the immune system or even parasites hold the key to certain infections. Now we speculate on processes, and the microbiota and neurons within the brain.

Hippocrates said; 'Men ought to know that from nothing else but from the brain come the joys, delights, laughter, sports and sorrows, griefs, despondency and lamentations… by the same organ we become mad, delirious, fearful. Terrors assail us.' We still are not sure how.

Maybe he should have added love to his list of things that arise in the human brain. What would Amelia say? Eros according to Socrates was a feeling for, and a contemplation of the beloved. Perhaps it is a way to see Amelia's soul. Am I capable of seeing what is sacred? I thought at that moment there was something wrong with me. I wanted nothing but good for Amelia yet here I am flirting with Mrs. G.

I am uninitiated. Yet we have always sought initiation. Disease, said Hippocrates, is sometimes described as men crying out, suffocating.

So he describes his anatomy of the brain. A patient's pain is not always located in the same spot on or in his or her head. Veins from the body's organs connect to the brain varying in size. Veins running along the right region of the body are described to the best of his knowledge: "The other runs upward by the right veins in the lungs and divides into branches for the heart and the right arm. The remaining part rises across the clavicle to the right side of the neck, so as to be seen; near the ear it is concealed, and there it divides; its thickest, largest, and most hollow part ends in the brain; another small vein goes to the right ear, another to the right eye, and another to the nostril." Like the horse painter Stubbs, Hippocrates learned physiognomy from the living *and* the dead, life and death sometimes barely separated.

He summarised symptoms which have echoes of the Covid pandemic.
- Shivering
- Loss of speech
- Trouble breathing
- Contraction of the brain
- Blood stops circulating
- Excretion of phlegm

All but for the last of these might also be symptoms of love. If this is true can disease itself be a window on the soul, and a pathway to God? Those afflicted with disease sometimes know it is coming. That is not true of love, although some do get confused and hide. What caused the flourishing of cranial surgery by the Greeks, also others long before them, witness the remains of ancient skulls? With the search for cranial remedies, there emerge processes for example in Bosnia.

What cures are there for love? For failing to love?

These terrors might pursue me even into sleep. I woke Mrs G.

'Cranial trepanation,' I said was first recorded by Hippocrates.

'So pleased,' she replied.

The Greek Theophanes mentioned revelations. 'What do you think?'

'Did this Theo read Arabic?' she asked.

'No idea, but good point.

Mrs Goldiwallah sat up, rubbed her eyes unsparingly, stretched, and then reported her own research findings. 'Today in Pakistan the brain is disturbed by stress according to fifty one per cent of respondents. Then thirty eight per cent describe abnormal electrical discharges in the brain. Only eleven per cent don't know. Pakistan is not behind the times. But I for one believe in possession too'

'Go Pakistan,' I cried. 'Maybe the Wing Commander is troubled by a minute distortion in the brain like a tiny speck of bone. What do you think?'

'Now is time,' she said, 'to come back to earth from your researches. Either the Wing Commander is possessed or he is not. When I was a girl I learned English. Here is a Welsh poem from 1600. I was forced to memorise it by colonial despots.

She recited:

'If thou canst get but thither, there grows the flower of peace,
The rose that cannot wither, Thy fortress, and thy ease.
Leave then thy foolish ranges, For none can thee secure,
But One, who never changes, Thy God, thy life, thy cure.

And here is a Persian poem,' she said, 'It is 400 years older than the Welsh and more mystical. I will recite first in Farsi then in English.' And she broke into a language I am not conversant with, and favoured me with a translation.

Not Christian or Jew or Muslim, not Hindu
Buddhist, Sufi, or Zen. Not any religion
or cultural system.
I am not from the East
or the West, not out of the ocean or up
from the ground, not natural or ethereal, not
composed of elements at all. I do not exist,
am not an entity in this world or in the next,
did not descend from Adam and Eve or any
origin story. My place is placeless, a trace
of the traceless. Neither body or soul.
I belong to the beloved, have seen the two
worlds as one and that one call to and know,
first, last, outer, inner, only that
breath breathing human being.

Now give over, she said. Will you?

She was really an extraordinary piece of work was Mrs Goldiwallah. You may by now find my interest in her disconcerting, but I am single minded in pursuit of intelligence, and as a spy I find it.

CHAPTER ELEVEN

On we went to Bahla where we met a man called al-Akmar. He knows a Djinn who lived under the ground there, and whose name sounded a bit like Niall (of the nine hostages.) Born of smokeless fire he dwells in dark unclean places in the fort of the Banu Nebhan, where they drove out ghouls and spirits who lure innocents into the deserts nearby. These become victims when their hearts do not properly recognise the power of God, said Mr al-Akmar.

The essence of the ritual of Zar is to coerce the spirit temporarily to come out and across into the medium, and then make it reveal why it possessed the victim in the first place, before we exorcise it.

Mr al-Akmar said he had met several Djinns, always at night in lonely places. 'Not that I get lost round here much,' he said, 'since I was born nearby. But I met one who took me off the beaten track to where one of these little trees grow decked out with plastic bags. Very beautiful, aren't they? This Djinn recruited me by promising to cure me of my thirstiness, which in the summer is very useful. He had some small bottles empty, or rather he filled these bottles with something. From the taste it could have been perfume. Anyway, they looked like perfume bottles and he made me drink them. They were sort of mixed with Fanta and Pepsi Cola. I fell asleep and when I woke up, I did not know where I was and it took me hours to get home in the dark.'

'I know what you mean about getting thirsty,' I said. 'Carrying this easel around me has me hot and bothered.'
    'Other Djinns have offered me lovely things too,' Mr al-Akmar went on. 'They gave me a mobile phone, male cosmetics,

a mirror, and, shameful but not entirely unwelcome, a Woman. Then when daylight comes they vanish by their magical powers. Their plan is to destroy us, but thankfully we have the Prophet, blessed be his name, and the great God Allah defends us. Iblis will be vanquished,' he said with conviction. 'One of my sons was possessed by a Djinn,' he continued 'but we have a man who drove the Djinn out of him.'

'This is where Zar comes in. I know what you want to ask. How is this done? This is a secret, and we cannot say for we have been sworn to keep this a secret. But I know. I know. He did this by the power of the Koran. I can tell you this at least. Pray five times a day, be clean and learn the Koran. Then every morning is a beautiful day around here.'

I half agreed with him.

The thing about desert is its pointlessness, I thought. *Perspective is one problem. Metaphor another.* Metaphorically, it is a prophecy of degradation. All this lifeless rubble, mostly sand, be it grey or ochre, be it salt and crystals, is the final outcome of remorseless processes that have, over aeons and aeons, minced everything into inert and terrible entropy. It invokes eviscerated space in which the refuse of history lies about, desperate and meaningless. It is the metaphor of our planet in which life is going extinct and only sadness lies before us.

'It depresses me,' I said.

'What's the matter now?' asked Mrs Goldiwallah.

'Soon the wilderness will be nothing but a very few extant specimens,' I replied. 'At your hands genocide after genocide of species are erasing all signs of life. Man himself is the last refugee. Man and Nature walk hand in hand into oblivion. A few microbiota may, like little Che Guevaras, attempt a rear-guard action, but it is hopeless.'

'But what about those goats over there?'

'Goats? What does this place mean to them? When I was at school a teacher explained that a landscapes of brilliant light and blackest shade shape strong characters and extreme and polar moods. I don't see it like that. I see dull grinding poverty of choice, poverty of outlook which breed oppression, and mad looking goats.' Mr al-Adami does not look too impressed. 'People,' I said, 'can fall into a cycle of credulity violence revenge, death. That's what deserts do. I should know. I look at one every morning. At a certain point the inhabitants rise up against us for failing to make things better.'

'Maybe it's time you took some leave,' said Mrs Goldiwallah. 'A little holiday perhaps.'

'For so many people the solution to the world is the sword.'

'Oh that? You mean the Khanjar!' she said.

'Once defeated, as inevitably they are, by perfidy or fate, what can they turn to? More sword. The sword demands obedience. Then all they can practice is sword or submission. If you are creative, hate and revenge get walk on parts. If not, hate and revenge become the stars.'

'No, no, retreat into religion and nurture it. What's got into you?'

'But what if the fuel is death. VS Naipaul on the invasions of Sind, that's your part of the world. Vast hordes mad for victory. So he wrote. And in the end long and terrible slaughter. Victory vindicates someone's version of the truth, there's no denying that. And it sows the idea that a sword explains everything. It doesn't though. Where is the room on a sword for progress? For freedom? true freedom of thought? for invention? Where is creative revolution and disruption? Where is imagination to refresh the tired and hungry spirit? Where are the creative ones that dance through history? They are not in the desert. There is no artist here.

'Maybe there is love? Where does George W Bush fit in?'

'Look at this place. Those great dunes. Funereal greys and in strong light shadows of intense blackness. See where the sand writhes like a living serpent its body, pewter, its skin rippling with striations of light, its forceful waterfalls of plummeting sand. Can you sense the sky at its zenith booming gunmetal blue and at its margin cyan and verdigris and turquoise. Look at those stacks of white pearl. Re-imagine them as waves. Look at that scree, which now supine relapses into the sea-less beach, catching spasmodically the slashing wounding light, or sucking our sins into holes of lapis lazuli. This inland sea of dry lethality deserves a proper name: axeinos, bitter, un-welcoming. That distant ambiguous horizon is a prospect of dangers; vast moving hordes or a solitary sinister messenger. And close out of the corner of the eye again and again a bloom of soft colour like algae vanishing when challenged by a direct gaze. Cyanobacteria I think decorate the imagination and even penetrate the gut brain axis perhaps by the vagus nerve until taking residence in the mind it subtly changes protein folding, and lays down a base for mournful Alzheimer's. I must reserve judgement on that because it is mostly cobbled together from things Amelia says.

'I don't understand,' said Mrs G. 'But if you feel fanciful why not invoke the colour schemes of your English paradise which is green.'

'This isn't the empty quarter,' I said. 'There are if you look acres of snowdrops fashioned out of pebbles, and deep drifts of white, fashioned out of suffocating dirt.'

'Well, paint it.'

'Few painters could turn this place into paradise. Daubigny, Claude, Cezanne. And of course there is Van Gogh. Did you ever see his *Road with Cypresses?*'

'I think so,' she said. 'Isn't there a big cypress in it?'

'The sun whirls and spins. The clouds pulse in vortices of passion. The road flows thick with ridges of white paint much like the scree flowing this way and that before you. And bang in the middle Van Gogh paints in a most unartistic way your big cypress, a shimmering swaying big cypress. Chop that down and you have the makings of a very good painting. But no one has come up with anything adjacent. Perhaps Soutine or Kossov. I may do one day.'

'Oh yeah?' she said ironically. 'But in one thing you are mistaken,' she explained. 'The cypress symbolises the beloved. Because it is tall and upright and because it never changes, you must never chop it down.'

This irritated me. At this point Mr al-Adami left us, mystifyingly.

I set up my easel. And rapidly began to paint.

The result I gave to Mrs G as a token of my esteem. But I could tell she was underwhelmed.

After we returned from Oman, I felt even more depressed by One Star's murder. I had not done enough to save him. He was not least of men, but in his way the greatest. I felt about him what one feels for the closest of friends. I went to visit the Wing Commander. My aim was to reconnoitre his supposed illness. His wife, meeting me at the door, appeared quite carefree. When I asked about his health, she gave the thumbs up. I was furnished with a cup of tea and shortly afterwards the Wing Commander joined me. His wife, making her excuses, left.

'I'll get to the point,' I said 'Do you know Amelia is here?'

'Amelia? No. Is she? What a nice surprise.'

'She and her supervisor are here on business. Have you met him? Very nice man. Professor Hughes Hallett. You would like him. I know you would. They have taken an apartment at al Qusais.'

'I didn't realise you knew her', he said. 'Why don't we have dinner? Sadly, my wife is going back to England tomorrow, to look after her mother. But we could have a threesome?'

'Why not? Could we make it early? I have a little illness. I am not drinking and mostly taking early nights. until they sort it out.'

'I am sorry. Will you have to be hospitalised?'

'No, no. A little examination. A test or two. Have you read *The Idiot*? Would you like a tea biscuit? I brought them from the UK with my Marden gin.'

'*The Idiot*? I tried to read it ages ago. Too much like hard work.'

'Prince Myshkin experienced bliss. His whole being opened up to a wonderful feeling of light, joy and hope, and all his cares were swept away. Actually, I think he saw God. That interest you?'

'Like falling in love?' I said. 'I did once. With Amelia actually.'

'Oh? Really? Do we have that in common? What a coincidence. Mrs Goldiwallah told me you are meeting in Ras al Khaimah tomorrow. Bit off your beaten track, isn't it?'

'I'm meeting Amelia, and Roy Hughes Hallett. Their idea actually. Didn't Mrs G say? Anyway you were telling me about this aura?'

'These moments are presentiments of the final second (never more than a second) in which joy comes upon you, before …'

'Death?'

'No. The aura. The fit comes later, like a train. Coming fast. Sometimes I actually smell burning, oleander perhaps?'

'That poisonous. How frightening. Poor you. How often?'

'Sometimes nothing for months on end. In fact I don't know too much at the time. It's in the aftermath when people talk to you. It hasn't affected me at all in the real world. But it is a surprise when someone comes up to you and says are you alright now?'

'How lovely to have that. What do you remember?' I asked.

'It gets harder to describe. They say it affects artists and religious men. People with strong views like me. Heaven only knows I'm not religious. But I feel, not to put too fine a word to it, exalted. And what Americans call psychedelia, wonderful bright colourful moments and great subtleties of tone and shade. I am elated, experiencing the sublime. Didn't you say you paint? You would love it.'

'Then it arrives. It is the apocalypse, or my idea of it. The veil lifts. The Kaleidoscope shakes and revelation is on me. Don't want to make myself sound religious. I am definitely not. I'm more puritanical me.

Maybe I've taken a knock, got some bruises, embarrassed myself.'

'Although you do not see yourself as particularly religious,' I said, 'does this experience make you more or less of a believer.'

'Less I would say. Since it is clearly a physical defect it would be too ironic if religion turns out to be a product of dysfunction. The likelihood is that it can be ameliorated by some pharma or another.'

'It sounds as if we don't actually know,' I said. 'Maybe it just opens a window, a sort of ceremony – I don't want to disparage. I might come to the conclusion we are hard wired to God. That would get my vote.'

'No, no. It's just part of the way we are, as fallible helpless humans. The Americans are right as usual. Americans are very religious. It all depends on where you draw the line. Do you remember the verse from school, when a man confesses he cannot look love in the eye. And love says who made the eye but I? The punch line is 'I did sit and eat.' Remember that? It was written by a man called Herbert something. Ah. Herbert Jones that's it.'

'I like to look at myself as an individual,' he said, 'autonomous, brave, resilient, an individual. You are not a microbe, are you?'

'Funny you should say that,' I said. Because at this particular moment I did feel a bit like a microbe. Certainly a fallible human being. 'I *am* a microbe,' I said.

'Good Heavens. Have your friends been telling you to be wary of Americans?'

'Well...'

'Let me give it to you straight. The Earth is dangling on a golden chain. To all intents democracy is the road to Peace. Or else the Gulf, this gulf will descend to night and Chaos. We need America.'

'Well,' I replied, 'you deserve a proper answer. I am recently persuaded American democracy is flawed. Yes, there are American idealists. But Iran too has idealists. The whole country suffered a trauma dealt to it by America and Britain, which has not been exorcised. Yes, we dangle precariously on a golden chain. Heaven is peace, when humanity ceases warring and restores Nature. Here in the Middle East your pax Americana is an arrangement with Saudi and Israel, bringing them close together. But Saudi is Iran's sworn enemy. And Iran stands for the Shia masses who your Americans slaughtered. And to be blunt I have spent a lifetime safeguarding the pax Americana, but find that they are not really involved in pax. In other words, they are as addicted to domination as they are to molasses. Yet I am their peeping Tom.'

The Wing Commander put his hands together as if washing them.

'I've got a test for you,' he said. 'I believe there is a Mossad agent here, which I'm sure your Ruler will not welcome.' He handed me a piece of paper. 'Here is where he can be found,' he explained. 'I was going to suggest you round him up. But to be on the safe side why not contact him and make up your own mind on the matter. Now,' said the Wing Commander 'I am going to have a bit of a lie down. Do let yourself out or failing that the Filippino maid will look after you.'

Whether the Wingco had a disease I did not know. Anyway in all innocence I took up his challenge.

I went looking for the maid to show me out. I stuck my head in a door and who should be there but Sacha and her sister Penelope.

'Hello girls,' I said.

'Hello Research Department,' said Sacha.

'Where is your maid?'

'Out. Buying us ice cream.'

'Well,' I said, 'I'll wait a while. Not watching television then?' They shook their heads sadly.

'Would you like a story then? There's only me. One Star is no more.'

'Yes,' they said, but I could tell they were only being polite.

So, we all sat down on the sofa and off I went.

'Once upon a time there was the most beautiful princess ever.'

They looked leerily at one another.

'Her name was Dawn. Now it happened she saw in the early light a man and fell in love with him.'

'But? said Sacha.

'He was overawed by her beauty and her name. Dawn decided to put a spell on him. She applied to the greatest Magus in the world and begged him to use his egromantic skills.'

'The Magus asked why she wanted this man, for how long, in what health, and so on and so forth. He was a magician and the most powerful lord of those times.'

'The Prince fell in love. She bore him two little boys, Memnon and Arithmaticon, only, unusually in Homer, Memnon was black.'

'Then one morning she noticed a line on her husband's forehead. And a single grey eyelash amongst the black. He could no longer lift his feet neatly off the ground. His memory declined. He had a permanent cold and his teeth rotted and fell out.' As I said this I found I was thinking of Amelia and the Wing Commander.

'But their son grew fine and tall and gathered a huge army of Indians and Africans and sailed to Troy and fought for King Priam.'

'Achilles, the greatest warrior the world has ever seen, slew him. A bird, a robin I think it was, came to the window and told his ageing father that Dawn and Memnon were an item. Though yearning for revenge, he died inwardly and became a cicada.'

'What do you think,' I said. 'She advertised for a husband, isolated him; watched him in fine detail, and within two years fell out of love. That is par for the course. One explanation is that you girls must try to be loyal. Utterly loyal. Nothing else counts.'

The girls were bored and were playing with their iPhones.

I wandered off depressed. Still, I said to myself. they are only young. Not enough blood and guts or sex.

The Wing Commander had fooled me. Sometimes you know when you've met your match. I rang the Israeli guy.

I met him, a very good looking dude, in a shabby place built in the sixties, completely out of keeping in the Emirates. The aircon was not working. He ushered me into a room furnished in sixties UK furniture.

What happened next was too fast for me. He whipped my arm up in a half nelson and frisked me. He found nothing. Dusting off my jacket he sat me down.

'Boy you're lucky. I was asked to rub you out.'

'Who by? What for?'

'You can't afford that information.'

'You can't afford to run amok round here.'

'No-one to stop me. This neighbourhood is defenceless. Your ruler pays you shit to keep it nice. I don't know what you do, but it doesn't amount to shit.'

'You're not working for the ayatollahs?'

'If I did you'd be toast.'

He removed my trousers stuck two letters on my backside, along with some cotton wool and tape to stop it showing and said: 'I don't want to see or hear from you again. You know where I come from. You're only hope is that you aren't branded un-American. Then you would have to wake up. Be professional. Be aware. Like standing over water, and seeing a huge sky and your own pathetic, solitary reflection below. Then wake up to how small you really are. Then you dive down and, if you don't drown, come back up into meaning. Get it?'

'No,' I said, playing devil's advocate, you mean like being held under, to learn my own secrets. Only if I submit will you know whether humiliation, pain, death were worth the finding out. Or is that too negative?'

'A philosopher eh? You're an amateur I can tell. I haven't got time for this. I just smell something wrong with you. Think hard. There are inside us visions and dreams. Heaven and hell. All senses, sights, smells, sounds have an otherworldly reference. If the smell is foul it must have its full origin in your mind. I don't need to tell you, but people round here have no notion of how much evil has grown. These people in Gaza. Violence is the cornerstone of their belief. But our people dying in Israel are real. You being what you are, you cannot see it.'

'I deal mostly with Iran,' I said. 'Your enemy. The Iranians are revolutionaries. Those who resent your axis of America and Saudi are drawn to supporting Iran and its proxies.'

'What are you saying?'

'A new world order. Revolutionaries resent colonialism. Any axis which feeds on power, money, privilege, is insensate to humanity.'

It was then that my eyes opened. A lifetime of supporting America fell away. My illusions vanishing, I thought of that film *One Life* when this man rescued children out of Czekoslovakia. My heart went out to them. *America was as foreign to them as Saudi.*

I was thrown out the door. I came away in a state of shock. To keep myself busy I sought out Amelia and arranged for her to meet Esa. It didn't work. Esa was ingratiating, trying to make a good impression. Amelia allowed him room to engage but Esa's conversation is no better than hers. One side is never right if the other is never wrong. So they circled one another inconclusively.

I took the long way out by delivering a lecture. 'Islam,' I said 'capitalised on Greek thinking.'

'You mean things thought two thousand years ago? asked Esa.

'A thousand years later medicine took root in Europe,' said Amelia.

'Yes,' I said approvingly. 'Europe became immensely competitive. Florence competed with Milan and Pisa. The Normans descended through Europe conquering, expropriating. The holy Roman Emperor fought with France. Spain fought off the Moors; and won parts of Italy. Aragon wrestled in Italy and with France. France fought England. Everywhere new minds germinated, then grew: Tycho de Brahe in Denmark, Copernicus in Poland, Kepler in Germany. The fizzing popping of bottles uncorked announced repressions, but again and again, freedoms. The fighting was all of a part of this fizzing and increased the ferment.'

'We tend to exaggerate,' said Amelia to Esa apologetically.

'Much of this was revolutionary,' I said, 'like Iran, but more inventive. The Muslims systematised knowledge. The Middle East split into divergent paths of recorded history. Later, directives began to drain the culture and ossify command structures and bureaucracies. But not so much in Persia,' I added in deference to Esa.

'After nearly eight hundred years the fall of Byzantium put paid to Rome. The winners inherited the remnants of the sultanate of Rum.'

'Islam was not affected,' said Esa. 'The Koran could not be changed.'

'The great Islamic multinational slowed to walking pace under mighty Turkic management, intent on conquest.'

'The Turkic people are good,' Esa said crisply.

'But the Book is omniscient. Revolution is superfluous.'

'Oh it is,' said Esa.

'The brain,' said Amelia, 'is looked at by the West through the lens of science. We go further: we use ignorance as a guide to discovery. This is a mulch from which new ideas spring. Creativity even now is breaking through existing paradigms. Feminism is one such revolution.'

'Yes, yes.' I added, 'in our terms, art, theatre, fiction can be used as disruptors to conventional thinking.' But then worried that we might seem to be ganging up I added, 'The best equipped in the Middle East were you Persians. Your culture, though resented by the Greeks came to lead in democracy and revolution. You established a leadership role amongst the Shia. You love poetry even more than your neighbours. You are worthy of deep respect. Your culture cannot be denied. Isn't that right Esa?'

'Not completely,' said Esa.

'Iranians differ from the axis, of Saudi and America, both materialist Magogs. Isn't that so, Esa?'

'I do not know Magog.'

'Iran stands for disruption of the oppressor and for the protection of the oppressed, in a good way,' I said ingratiatingly.

CHAPTER TWELVE

The Wing Commander left a message: he could not attend the meeting. Then out of the blue Mrs Goldiwallah came into my office and putting her index finger to her lips, said, 'I have a little visitor.'

'Come in, come in,' I cried as she ushered in Sacha. 'What a nice surprise. Would you like a Fanta?'

'No thank you,' she replied. 'I hope you don't mind but I am after some information.

'Of course.'

'Perhaps you've heard my Dad's not too well.'

'I saw him the other day. He'll be all right, I'm sure. What's up?'

'I heard him through the door arguing with mummy. He said she must work harder at it.'

'At what?'

'I don't know. That's the problem. He said he realised things weren't as they seemed. What with me having two mothers. Do you know what that means?'

'No, I can't say I do. How's your school work going?'

'Quite well actually. I have written a story, so won't get my head chopped off. Remember?'

'Yes, of course. Who could forget?

'The story goes like this: When from my dust a blood red flower is rising, on each green branch a nightingale will sing. And underneath Salsabil's stream is flowing.'

'That *is* lovely.'

'Have you heard of Salsabil's sweet stream?'

'No, I haven't actually.'

'The story is about Farhad and Shirin the beautiful daughter of the Emperor of Byzantium. It's like Romeo and Juliet but worse. They each commit suicide thinking the other one is dead. It's Persian.'

'Oh, my poor dear child,' I said.

Later Mrs Goldiwallah by her own unique reasoning arrived at the Ritz Carlton at Ras al-Khaimah in search of the Wing Commander. She squinted at the three dark buildings which sulked in monotonous high rise mode in the distance. Designed no doubt by expensive architects, they rose like broken teeth beyond the lagoon, in no way less deficient, than their grim forebears in Sheffield. And there was the Wing Commander just as she anticipated, seated in the shade next to the swimming pool.

'Wing Commander!' I cried. 'What brings you so far off the beaten track? Must be pretty special, eh Wing Commander?'

'Eh? Oh fidget. I mean good lord you gave me a shock. It's little Mrs Goldiwallah isn't it? I have a sense of déjà vu. Funny old world.'

'A coincidence?'

'I like to keep up with developments, particularly luxurious ones, so I thought I'd take a closer look at the Carlton,' he said, closing his book.

'Are you safe in this pitiless sun?'

He looked irritated. 'Oh that,' he said, 'it is nothing. Actually, I have an appointment later on today to see a specialist. I have a Mustang to shoot me into town. What brings you here?'

'Is it nice here? I know so little, being just a country girl.'

This won a sardonic glare. 'It is too difficult to explain,' he replied. Technically it is my temporal lobe. No lasting after effects in my case.'

'That sounds like good news. It's harmless then?'

'Science, I learned recently, has found how to trigger it. Now everyone is prone to fall down. Whole armies unmanned.'

'You up for those kinds of fun and games? Lucky I bumped into you.'

'Oh?'

'Are you religious then?'

'No. Why the devil do people keep asking this? I lived for a while in the Bible belt and found their worship satisfying. No, I'm not religious. I'm off anything that leads to overexcitement.'

'Off games then?'

'I have reserved a room here so I may lie down. So if you will excuse me. If you get hot you're welcome to join me upstairs for a cup of tea.'

At this point he seemed to have tears in his eyes. 'I have to dash off to the Research Department,' I replied. 'Speedy recovery Wing Commander. God bless. I hope to see Amelia. Shall I give her your best? Inshallah.'

'I blew him a kiss and hastily departed. It was already 40 degrees. Thank God for Nippon aircon,' she wrote. 'Is he up to no good? I am sure he is. He more or less confessed to being possessed. Even if he wasn't he s bound to go through with the abduction, because possessed or not he is has been bought by America.

Meanwhile I was taking a nap, and later awoke from a troubling dream. Amelia was in it. We were arguing over how to master a Djinn.

My memory of the dream was evaporating.

A prophet was there. 'Is Amelia around? he asked.

'The decisions are hers,' I replied. 'There is no bond she cannot break, though breaking them diminishes her.'

'You are awake you know,' he said. And I began to recall her high seriousness in comparison to my own trivial behaviour in the past. I remember her careful plotting and planning often on my behalf.

Her commitment contrasts with my instincts which flower and wilt on the smallest pretext. At one stage she had faith in me. She took me seriously. I did not. Her seriousness was born of her own self-belief. Why she now thaws a little in her dealings with me I do not know. I used to despise her conformity. I admit to my waywardness. For example, I give in to dark thoughts. It occurs to me that Evil holds the trump cards. An evil dictator has less constraints than a good man. Evil unconstrained is more imaginative, often more successful. I struggle to identify how or why good men might win. In reality leaders who win can have in their psychology something dangerous and cruel. I have created hurt, then nursed my own. I must change.

I was on my third cup of coffee when Mrs Goldiwallah came in.

'I know he's guilty', she said. 'I checked with hotel reception. He booked the room not just for today but for tonight as well. Our analysis is correct. What a hypocrite. He lived in the Bible belt once.'

'Which means?'

'He has a hyper personality. The geshwind syndrome includes sexuality. I was watching out, believe me.'

'*Déjà vu* suggests electric bursts in the temporal lobe.' I said, trying to sound expert.

'The full works?'

'Anxiety? Fearfulness? Fainting? Paranoia? Cheating? Accusations? Then there is postictal psychosis post seizure. Did you notice nose wiping, fidgeting, blinking? All good signposts. Apparently.'

'No, no sign at all.'

'Could he understand what you were saying? There is a separate place for language called Wernicke's area, usually on the left.'

'Fascinating. No. He did say f***. Surprisingly. I thought. For him.'

'Hearing someone swear doesn't just activate Wernicke's area but also the insula structure in the limbic system. In the insula disgust is registered. So much for relativism. The limbic system and insula determine moral outrage. I know this thanks to Amelia.'

'Goodness, she is a fount of knowledge.'

Spontaneous swearing implicates the amygdalae and the basal ganglia in the production of swear words –the amygdalae and basal ganglia have a role in control and aggression; the basal ganglia involve a group of neurons deep in the cerebrum. Their role is impulse control. Hopefully.'

'Well, never mind. I think the time has come to mobilise MacSpity and his leprechauns. Let's synchronise. Hughes Hallett and Amelia will arrive at the Ritz Carlton in half an hour.'

'We've arranged a car to pick them up at 20.00 hrs. The Wing Commander will hijack Amelia after 20.30.'

'And MacSpity?'

'Should be on his way.'

'The Wing Commander is doomed,' said Mrs G. 'MacSpity's already there. He reports a high-speed craft docking in the environs with a crew of six US Navy Seals, as we speak.'

When I arrived, Amelia and Hughes Hallett were deep in conversation with the Wing Commander, who looked very smart in uniform.

I was nervous, steeling myself to do something unimaginable. I was going to betray Amelia again. How could I, after everything. How did this compute? But I will live with the consequences. My mind, is now ruled by reason. She will understand.

'My dear Amelia,'the Wing Commander was saying. 'It is completely unacceptable that you be coerced by anyone.'

'You have no say in the matter.'

'Here is Dylan. Dylan, there seems to be an awful mix up. The Iranians are trying to coerce these good people to make the crossing.'

'A coup?'

'Don't be alarmed,' he said sternly. 'What I'm going to do now is a rescue mission directing American personnel against illegal abduction.'

'My God,' said Amelia. 'Fuck you.'

Suddenly his voice turned into a parade ground order. 'No one move!' shouted the Wing Commander. 'A protective square will now be formed. We are being taken for our safety on board the destroyer.'

But just at this point MacSpity arrived in a truck with a number of large Baluchis in pyjama, some armed. They interposed themselves between the US Seals and Amelia so fast no-one had time to take off safety catches. Three of them rushed the Wing Commander.

'What?' he cries. 'Whoa!'

'The laws of the United Arab Emirates apply,' I shouted.

'The laws of the Ras al Khaimah apply,' shouts MacSpity ducking and weaving and kicking out.

'Where are we?' The muffled voice of the Wing Commander can be heard at the higher end of the scale, as he descends under a scrum of bodies. At this IRGC guys appear. Heavily armed, they chase off the squaddies of whom there are now pitifully few.

Two of the Seals retreat to their boat with Amelia.

The IRGC guys grab her for Iran.

Hughes Hallett, in a headlock, is re-engineered by pyjamas.

'And where are the so-called security forces?' says a voice.

'Ah Esa! Just in time. Talk to your IRGC guys. They've got her,' I shout.

Amelia, alarmed, cries. 'Where are they taking me?'

I shout back. 'You'll be safe. Esa here will keep an eye out for you. For what it's worth, this is America's doing.'

At this, sporadic gunfire breaks out. Hughes Hallett is wrestled away, crying emotionally. 'Amelia!'

MacSpity roars: 'Look out for the man in uniform. He's having a fit.'

'Are you sure?' I say, ill advisedly.

'I know one when I see one. Give him air. Dylan, get an ambulance.'

The American launch is empty. A fast Iranian boat swings out into the perfect moonlit sea. On it just discernible is Amelia. I just hear her. 'You shit,' she yells.

Esa comes over. 'Has the Research Department taken leave?' he asks.

'Are you not accompanying her, Esa?'

'Things are not that straightforward, boss,' he replies. 'Don't worry. I may not be safe just now. We are two different departments. IRGC do not recognise me. Truth is they do not like me. Don't worry. She will be taken to appointments efficiently, punctually.'

'What guarantee do we have she will be released?' I ask.

'None,' says Esa. 'She is a chip.'

'If she is mistreated, I will go after her.'

'Boss,' says Esa. 'In the real world you count for nothing. You made your mark. Do not punish yourself. A man of your age does not heal quickly.'

Suddenly I am breathless. 'Sa'ab, says a policeman. 'See this.'

A figure lies in the shadows. It is Mrs Goldiwallah. A tiny depression in her forehead reveals the cause of death. Why? How little I know her. I am utterly distraught.

CHAPTER THIRTEEN

I saw early on life that men are locusts.

Years ago, I met that Gujerati in the Edgware Road. In a café, since gone Arab, I asked, 'What is the country like in the Gulf? Is it eaten up? Is it a kind of waste?'

'Great palaces, ministries, and hotels are everywhere,' he replied. 'They measure progress by the barrels of oil poured into the sands. The future will be baffled by sudden flowerings of civilisation, deflowered.'

'How does it compare to Gujerat?'

'Our land is deep with the loam of history, in rich diversity, in art, in intellect and the spirit world. But for the greater part our people work on the land living pitiably.'

'Is the land so poor?' I asked him.

'It is dunged with the dung of men. But like all of India it fights bravely for survival, the survival of the Earth, who created us, who, so the Chaldeans say, *is* our mother.'

'Were you not born in Africa?' I said to prove him.

'Africa was my foster mother. During the British occupation,' he said, my people went there in search of work.'

'What did it mean to be Gujerati in Africa?' I enquired.

'Magnificent. We were enamoured of a thousand flavours. Uganda was heaven with so many delicious things to eat. It was creation as a mother provides it. My people were indentured, but in love.'

'I wonder if this did not warm them to Christianity?'

'Go to East Africa and then the Gulf and compare them,' he commanded.

'Why the Gulf?'

'If you are going to hell, learn to savour waste. The Chaldeans who taught the Greeks and the Arabs astronomy say the Earth, born in violence and pain, seeing her orphans die, weeps continuously.'

'Where would you pitch camp?'

'Sohar,' he said (which is where Mrs G and I had passed by later.)

But in the Edgeware Road, I asked him 'Is there work in Sohar?'

'For a man like you, why not? But' he said, 'my father in his youth planned to be a freedom fighter. Now his world is dying at the hands of the West. I am just a Gujerati. In the Middle East inequality is everywhere. Monotheists fight it out for supremacy; Nature goes hang.'

'But surely in India things are worse?'

'The thing about us is our heroism. India was colonised not once but many times. And despite this it has deep, deep roots further back than any civilisation. If you believe, as I do, that the past contains true wisdom then India is intact. Its colonisers are not. We are for the most part vegetarians, pioneers of nonviolence, anarchists and spiritual revolutionaries. Apart from Tolstoy the rest of the world are mere onlookers. Nature is on her knees but India from castes to famines, to her gods, is proud and natural.'

A seed was planted in my mind by this Gujerati. I came to associate India with Russia but without the cold sort of violence. A kind of idealistic anarchy which can save the world. A bypass. Does colonisation not lead to revolution whose children are pain and injustice. America gained independence then colonised its continent with cruelty and injustice. The real colonised. I suppose Iran thinks they have found a resolution. And what of Russia? At least it had belief but now is tainted and in need of spiritual restitution. Under current management it claims to have returned to Orthodox Christianity. Sooner or later with the help of friends it will discover its iniquity, and as a *massa damnata*, repent, learning that killing innocents is after all a sin, and that leaders of concupiscence are eternal sinners. Iran, Russia, America, Saudi worship oil. Saudi so much so that they are investing in contradiction to the fight against global warming.

In my cell in Teheran I fell ill and wondered if an epidemic was underway. My keeper allows Amelia to give me medicines and reading material.

I suppose the Iranians are trying to keep her sweet. She says that simple viruses properly administered can evade diagnosis. In Buraimi she had led me up the garden path. While we were there one thing led to another. 'You need to loosen up,' she said. 'Let me take you by the hand.' So she did. She was preparing a vaccination or at least some kind of injection. 'Imagine you are Huxley taking your first trip on mescaline or LSD,' she said. 'First, I will enable you to see. Next, I will open a door in your mind but do not worry. Everything is under control. We know the mechanisms to do the job; I have a drug therapy which can modulate or exacerbate inflammation. Is that not wonderful? Virus infections lead to activation of cell types, particularly macrophages releasing molecules that induce malfunction. If I choose not to inhibit viral replication we will see inflammation, a cytokine storm and acute respiratory distress. But I do not so choose. I want you to know more. I will lend you knowledge, but rest assured I will keep you well.'

I do not know how much of what she said was based on guess-work. But I know she is ethical. One hundred per cent.

When I arrived in Iran we were incarcerated in a high security prison. This confirmed that theology was afoot as well as science. I had to protect myself. I rehearsed what I knew from reading. I was frightened, as I knew some of the theocrats by report. I prepared myself. What did I know?

The Ash'arites believe God is the only cause, so the world is a series of events, each one willed by God alone. This pretty much puts paid to Amelia's science. The Persians boasted a history of research into medicine, and astronomy. My mental model of Islam is of a multinational. You conquer so many countries (as did the British), then you pick and choose and move around the best stuff from each territory you have won. You assess and amplify. Ash'arites believe the Koran is God's and therefore unchallengeable. As for Nature, God's will is sufficient. In other words, it is of limited value that Amelia should search for better or different answers than God's. Natural things appear permanent, but God wills every single atomic event, which is fair enough. This defies any attempt to explain the coherence of the natural world by Western science. Reason teaches us to discover, question, and innovate, so Reason is the enemy of scripture: "Nothing in nature can act spontaneously and apart from God," wrote Ghazzali. Natural disasters are a function of God's punishment of man which is fair enough.

All legal and moral enquiries are submitted. At this point the argument becomes circular. The authorities can't be questioned as they are God's chosen. This is almost as bad as the US Supreme Court. I apologise for rehearsing this, but I hope to explain my concerns about interrogation. In fact they turn out to be superfluous. My interrogator's line is more difficult to counter.

'Your employer,' he said, 'sent me an analysis of your character. He has asked me to tell you your employment is rescinded. You overstepped your terms of employment by preventing the female scientist from carrying out her proper task of debriefing our government.'

My next interview was with a man with a toothpick, who treated me as a modernist, beyond the pale, a spy, and a double agent.

'Saudi has chosen to be a Western nation,' he said. 'Even your Ruler is displeased. You have long been noted by us as a spy and an idolater. If we send you West, you die. If you stay in this cell you die.'

'What will you do with my scientist?' I said. 'How is she?'

'The Americans will decide. She is of little worth to us. She thinks her Huge Hallett is the saviour of the planet. If he lives, he can come and share science with us and maybe we will release her. But I think not.'

'They are two people who can prevent extinction,' I said.

'It is not for you to say. Extinction is the work of kaffirs. You are a kaffir.'

'Hughes Hallett has the credentials, worldwide. Who else is there? I do not know if I am kaffir. I know some who declare *you* kaffir.'

'You are an unbeliever.'

'Is that what she says? That I am an unbeliever?'

'No. She says you are a student of the Book and of the prophets.'

'She said that?'

'Are you devout?'

'I believe in God.'

'Not the prophets? That's what I thought. The scientist believes nothing. She discounts the prophets: I discount her. Her science is credible, she says, ask the Russians. A woman? Instructing us?'

'What does she say about the science?

'She can diagnose fits. She can prevent fits. She can trigger fits. She can unman America. Let her do these things before the ulama.'

'Her science is no less useful than nuclear.'

'God does not intend her to succeed. We protect her from herself. We will protect ourselves against the West, with nuclear. Why not with fits?

'I am glad.'

'That does not concern me, my friend. You have no job. Your Ruler has erased you from his kingdom. You have no woman. You have no value. Why are you here?'

I was going to ask the same question. Instead I said I will tell you what you want to know.

Alone in my cell I ask myself where did all my spying get me? One Star said America will break up, due to inequality, ethnic fragmentation, and their piss poor constitution. Locally my research centred on finding victims, watching them closely, occasionally trapping and isolating them, and then trying to get inside their heads. I felt I was getting there with the Wing Commander. I am a kind of Peeping Tom but the Wingco eluded me by deceit and strangely enough by being personable. He is no serial killer but leaves that to his superiors.

I fall back into the big picture. One Star claimed the world itself is disintegrating as old powers like Russia and new ones like Brazil and Saudi and retreads like America and Iran seek new ways to break the rules. And, said One Star, our planet at the very moment of acute danger, fails to cohere.

But each of these powers worships oil. Oil funds Iran against Israel and America. Saudi conspires with Russia to raise the oil price to cement their leadership and zenophobia. Supporters of Israel in America plot to bring down the price of oil to defang Iran. There is truly One great God; but these little powers, including America, live and die for oil, and worship the black shiny gods of oil. Once Gold did for Incas and Spaniards; Water did for Cambodia. Cycles of triumph and death will do for these worshippers of oil. The black oil gods face extinction. After a lifetime of proselytising for America I refute Edmund Burke. Britons and Americans never were one people. America discredited their revolution, and now ally themselves with Saudi. The French discredited their revolution. By each I am offended and alienated.

Left to my own devices in a small cell with poor hygiene I take to drafting a memoire inside my head (no pen, no paper). The title I decide on is Peeping Tom, peeping on people through my peephole. I was in great spirits thinking Amelia had spoken of me protectively.

Esa was brought in, presumably to spy on me, and induce a confession under the stress of fear. We were put into an even tinier airless room together with a frightened looking youngster who made notes.

'Your Americans are working to a plan,' Esa said, eyeing me suspiciously.

'The Americans did not want her here. I did,' I replied.

He looked uncertain. 'You are insincere,' he said. 'You had this coming. I am not your friend. Know this.'

'Oh, Esa.'

'The scientist loves you. She say so. But I do not estimate you. Now you have hope. Isn't it?'

'She loves me? Maybe. I always loved her. We do not train scientists in religion,' I explained.

'Does she believe?'

'I believe. She does not.'

'What does she want?'

'What does a mother want?'

'Obedience and love.'

'You know you have changed,' he said. 'Once you loved America.'

'Once I loved America. Now I am mad,' I replied.

Back in my dirty cell I wondered who really wanted Amelia here. Had a dirty deal been struck? Wrongly I had recused myself from controlling transits into Iran. I had refused permission to Hughes Hallet. The IRGC brought Amelia here with my acquiescence. What I have done endangers Amelia, favours Iran, and in a small way helps America with their feckless settler mentality.

I fell asleep and had a dream I was out at sea in the Gulf. This idea of being at sea, repeats itself. The light on the water is intense and strange. An aircraft carrier- it is American- sails over smaller craft. Fear precedes it; fear follows it. Fear envelopes it. There is no resistance.

I woke up. Esa was gently shaking me. 'Your sheikh is at work,' he said. 'He has found an ancient protocol to deal with the IRGC directly on matters of mutual concern.'

'Why did he let them take her?' I asked.

'God decides,' said Esa. 'IRGC and your sheikh are irrelevant as you are. It turns out your Amelia is a gift from America. *That's why the Wing Commander was involved,* I thought. America wants to get the Saudis back in line. Their logic is that Iran, as the champion of Shi'ites across the region, are a useful counterweight, but only within the vice-like grip of the American embargo. Iran has access to arms from Russia and North Korea, and even Turkey, with its age old aspirations. In the *s*ouks they notice when the IRGC lose control. Britain and Hughes Hallett will be seen as conspirators, and I, as small fry, will be blamed. Iran will renew their enmity, which is non-negotiable.

If Prince Salman is Alexander the Great then the Gulf is ancient Greece, I told Esa. He looked baffled. 'The locals,' I said, 'like Qatar, are squabbling, making war, manoeuvring, changing alliances, but with this difference. Alexander conquered Persia then India. The Prince despite his vast wealth can do neither. The Greek city states, even in Alexander's time were inventive, combative, creative. The Gulf states are not. Maybe Salman could stage a putsch somewhere within his reach. But what good would it do him? Alexander had Aristotle tutor him. The Prince does not want tutoring. He thinks he can outfox America. America thinks to outfox him. America will fail. They never learn'

'Maybe,' said Esa, 'the coup will start in America.'

'The world is shaped by coups, I replied. Coup after hidden coup. The EU piratically sails under a democratic flag, crewed year in year out by the unelected and undemocratic, under the eyes of a court fundamentally politicised. We know all about such coups in the West. We just don't discuss them. How then should we view the Middle East? Saudi leans towards Westernisation. It sails to its own materialist star. Its flotilla includes Israel, your sworn enemy. The Crown Prince, like

Israel, is safeguarded by America. I believe Saudi will attack you with American connivance. I will be liberated. So keep me healthy and yourself safe.

'That,' said Esa, 'is what we call 'make believe' Disney.'

'You are struggling,' I replied. 'You carry the brunt of American imperialism. Only China can rescue you. Why should they bother?'

'You forget Russia. Saudi needs America to control the Gulf and the Indian Ocean, and they need Russia to keep prices high. China will dispute both.'

Why am I debating with Esa? I thought. He knows nothing. The Gulf, despite its downtrodden masses, and the plutocracy of its ruling families, knows the time will come when Islamic power will be united, and make war as described in their book. This is what Ayatollah Khomeini wanted, on his terms. China will not, in the long term, allow America to have the Middle East. 'Esa,' I said, 'dear Esa, the Gulf was not created for America. Be patient. Pull in your horns.'

Amelia says she loves me. I realise that I love her hopelessly, just as I once did before. But I am mad.

'You are alone,' says Amelia. 'But I am with you forever.' Esa relays these vows, with histrionic passion.

Yet here I am in a land of prophets. The Book defines worship and does away with original sin just when it is needed desperately. We like to big up men beyond their design and beyond their capacity for selflessness. The intruder Constantine recruited gentle Jesus into the bureaucracy. Arguments multiplied. Augustine condemned babies unbaptised to go to hell; and male semen was identified as the means by which original sin was heritable, leaving only Jesus Christ, conceived without it, free. Augustine by this salvo unleashed an avalanche of despair so Pope Pius XI in his Casti connubii: could say: "The natural generation of life has become the path of death by which original sin is communicated to the children."

Prophets prophesy: some choosing to fall, some to envision, some to foam. Religion, alas, degenerated into marketing, segmentation, positioning, competitive claims and offers. Can we not go back to Aristotle to reaffirm free will, and rediscover the origins of sin?

I wonder is the Earth, suspended on its golden chain, capable of surviving our disobedience? Is the Gulf, where I have lived for many years, the abyss into which we must fall? Can the Chinese rescue us? They, who in the time of Ming, sent a vast fleet of a thousand junks to announce themselves at Ormuz?

In the last days Amelia (via Esa) revealed her recent work in secret messages to me. This centres on the Insula, the fabled region which hoards what is mystical in humanity.

There are few moments in the brain, very few, she says when there is no surprise, no unexpected electrical discharge, no surge of blood, but only deep certainty, resonance, and transcendence.

It comes about at the singular moment, she writes, when personal belief is mapped precisely on *the world outside*.

You are the world outside, she writes. This is the moment when love and ecstasy are born. This is when you above all, Dylan, will be strong. The Insula anterior predicts the future, calling up from memory your hopes, ideals, and passions.

I smile for I am made of them.

The Insula posterior checks this against what is happening as your senses are reporting it.

The prediction and the report rarely match. When prediction and the world outside do not match, your brain has two options; change the prediction; or change the world.

I have tried to change the world, I thought, but have failed. I changed and betrayed you, Amelia. That was a sin.

She replies that in such cases when the two do match; a *sudden calm* ensues. You will hear a still small voice; the ineffable is spoken; the mystical aura blows. Then a surge of ecstasy fires a quickening of your blood. Love and inspiration follow.

Those are the moments; when she could meet God.

Poor sweet Amelia is in Limbo. If only she could change forever. Love longing for unity, would seek consummation. I weep. I love her.

I continue to dream of the ship that commands the seas. It is immense and horrifying. Its name is Fortune. It was at Salamis and Trafalgar. It confers victory for the price of death. Victory is the prize that humans, parasites and microbiota crave. War is always with us. Americans are warlike creatures. Even in the way they feed children into it.

Though the good ship Fortune is on the horizon, America, when it embarked on its wars in Vietnam, Cambodia, Afghanistan and Iraq committed such crimes against humanity.

In the new era America makes the Chinese economy stronger. It has helped unify China. We do not know when America will fall, but its imperium is weakening. Its failure at conciliation, and collaboration is based on ignorance and condescension. Fortune awaits them.

The message is a warning; the aura precedes the storm.

I can see why in the absence of love and religion the Insula is a mimic.

When the soul's journey is mimicked, the aura is accompanied by changing brain activity. Signals of music, colour, smell, taste, nausea, and *déjà vu*, warn that change is under way. In the case of the diseased world the warning din is accompanied by new symptoms: heat waves, melting ice, changing sea levels. In the case of the Wing Commander he will lose consciousness, purging his mind of imperfections.

I am alone now, imprisoned, as we all are, I suppose. I foresee the end. Those who greet me will, I pray, be the very ones who have helped me in my search for truth, One Star and Amelia.

Gandhi, with his friend Tolstoy will greet me. Better than prophets, they are messengers of union.

Amelia has returned to England. She now does whatever she pleases.

'Did the Bible not save the world?' I once asked her.

'The opposite.'

'Has your science saved the world?'

'You tell me.'

'I say it is failing horribly. Darwin is execrable.

It was after this my symptoms appeared. We had gone on a Wadi bash in Oman. It was then under a clear blue sky I felt the world unhinge.

Yet looking back it was I unhinging. Nothing was normal. At one stage the Wadi, which lay before us like a river bed suddenly rose up vertically into the figure of a man and then the pebbles the stones and rocks sprang up as dogs and deer, so vividly did the wild rise from the ground. And the boulders the size and the propensity of bears towered and threatened me. It was only after pleading with Amelia that I composed myself. Ever since then I have taken to recalling the footpath which runs beside the Nailbourne beneath black poplars along the Elham valley. The footpath rises in my imagination, and like the Wadi takes the shapes of beasts, as textured and coloured and decorated as the path itself in every detail of leaves, twigs, grasses, nettles and fallen branches. Then I rejoice to be in Nature. But doubts assail me. What if these visions are untrue. But as they invoke Nature I am comforted. What I see is rare and privileged. If there is deceit it is of my making. The things I see are natural.

It was after this that something happened to my hearing. I hear sounds of a bear roaring; and of what I take to be innumerable locusts consummating their destiny.

My memory is untethered and hyperactive as if everything in the world is supernatural; strange music, outside my cell, colours, smells, tastes, and in my mouth, sickness, all surreal.

As for captors I forgive them. Do they not struggle to match God's will?

The storm impends.

I was summoned again to be interrogated.

'We have considered you, they said. You make Islam your concern. But you are mistaken. Such arrogance is American, but they fail as you will fail. Israel is theirs. It daily colonises. And through Riyadh America hopes to control the Middle East. They cannot. Israel makes settlement after settlement defying the world. America pretends to oppose this but supports it.'

'Islamic unity will come,' I said.

'You know nothing. Why are you blind? America uses Saudi as a weapon against us. But they are doomed. The Chinese plan for fifty years. They are long sighted. The Americans are trapped. We know everything about you.'

'How?'

'Your Personal Assistant spied for us over many years. He is a great man. He has got us to improve relations with Turkey, and India. He is tirelessly helping to replace the UN, the IMF, the World Bank with institutions that represent the majority, not America. He regards the veto system in the UN with contempt.'

'How does he influence you?'

'By teaching how to take power. He will save the planet. You hate him?'

'No, I love him and respect him.'

I dream of freedom. Spying has imprisoned me. It was Amelia's mother made me a spy. She judged me and taught her daughter I was unfit. She demasted me. She showed I was an outsider, the stuff a mere spy is made from. Someone unable to stand on his own two feet; to compete out in the open, to show strength in confrontation, and composure in society. She divorced her husband who in other respects had made a name for himself. To her men had to prove themselves in the eyes of her confidants. So I insinuated myself into society and unpicked my enemies behind their backs. Dissimulation, pretence, secrecy, and my tireless dismantling of others offered solace. Mother and daughter watched as I struggled, friendless. I on the outside, looking in, with neither wit nor ambition to lead others, preferred to lie in wait; to break into the lives of unsuspecting victims, under cover of darkness. Eventually I insinuated myself into the company of big senseless men that is to say America, and bought their propaganda. Of course I saw them differently then; I saw them as idealists. I overlooked the boorishness, the greed, the violence.

Amelia back then was objective, cold, and cautious. She saw that her mother had been let down by a careless father, who, leaving home in disgrace, was, in his absence, excoriated by his wife.

And my poor dear Amelia, bright, ambitious, good at science, confident and hopeful, planned an independent future in which her blustering mother could impose her social pretences only occasionally, and could tax goodness and idealism only at the risk of her daughter's silence.

Her Mother came on strong, and trained her daughter daily to flirt with her, and play the little child, a child who must hide, obey, and wait. Although Amelia saw me as weak she could remodel me. When I rebelled she was disgusted. Then I betrayed my Amelia, dedicating my life to America, and promoting their ideals only to betray them also. I was, after all, a well trained spy.

I fell ill again. Esa visited

'Oh by the way,' he says 'Your Personal Assistant asks after you.'

'He is dead.'

'I met him in Abu Dhabi.'

'How can that be?'

'It is so.'

I wept. According to Esa, One Star has returned.

'If he is alive, does he know I'm here?'

'He sends good wishes.'

'But what did he say?

'I did not understand him. He thinks Gandhi was the greatest of all. Yet Gandhi said the British Empire was a benefit to the world. Your Personal Assistant wants to subjugate us all.'

'Dear One Star. Back from the dead. Don't take offence, Esa, but slaughter and the destruction of holy places, reawaken terrible memories. It is not the right or wrong of Aurangzeb at issue, but the trauma, which survives, a creature in its own right. The recent slaughter in Iraq is like the slaughter at the hands of Timur. As for Aurangzeb the weight of history broke his empire as the weight of history now weighs upon America. They have no get out of jail card to play.'

'Who is in jail?'

'Me. Am I not? And they send you to spy on me. Are the trees in leaf outside?' I asked.

'You have been in here too long,' Esa sighed. 'Now Satan is attacking us. He has made the region a waste. What trees?'

'Trees where songbirds flute. They are the seat of human souls. I have seen your Tree of Life, scarlet against a sky of pure blue silk. The Jews also have a Tree of Life. They taught us scripture and one God. Are we not all interconnected?'

'We have such trees,' said Esa, 'like oak, pomegranate, almond, peach, walnut, fig. The West attacks Nature. We offer hope. Without heaven man will not save the Earth. In the end all will be resurrected and judged. Then we will know the end of days. America has lost control. The money. The weapons. The conspiracies. They have lost control of Israel. What will your One Star do now?' he asked

EIN HERZ FÜR AUTOREN A HEART FOR AUTHORS À L'ÉCOUTE DES AUTEURS MIA ΚΑΡΔΙΑ ΓΙΑ ΣΥΓ
HJÄRTA FÖR FÖRFATTARE UN CORAZÓN POR LOS AUTORES YAZARLARIMIZA GÖNÜL VERELIM S
CUORE PER AUTORI ET HJERTE FOR FORFATTERE EEN HART VOOR SCHRIJVERS TEMOS OS AU
SERCE ZÖINKÉRT SERCE DLA AUTORÓW EIN HERZ FÜR AUTOREN A HEART FOR AUTHORS À L'ÉCO
RAÇÃO BCEЙ ДУШОЙ К АВТОРАМ ETT HJÄRTA FÖR FÖRFATTARE Á LA ESCUCHA DE LOS AUT
EURS MIA ΚΑΡΔΙΑ ΓΙΑ ΣΥΓΓΡΑΦΕΙΣ UN CUORE PER AUTORI ET HJERTE FOR FORFATTERE EEN
YAZARLARIMIZA GÖNÜL VERE ZÖINKÉRT SERCE DLA AUTORÓW EIN HERZ FÜ
OR SCHRIJVERS TEMOS OS AÇÃO BCEЙ ДУШОЙ К АВТОРАМ ETT HJÄRTA FÖ

The author

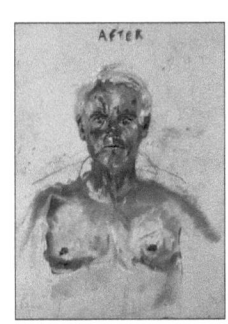

Born in High Beech, Essex in 1941, Alex Troy grew up on the tropical island of Trinidad and in the Port City of Hamburg Germany, where he saw first hand the hardship of life and the tenacity and ambition it takes to survive. He studied classical literature at Oxford, worked in Dublin and Belfast in the 1970s, then in the Middle East and Africa. Father of three and now retired in Kent he pursues his interest in painting, fiction, and his border terrier Agatha.